A DAY IN NOVEMBER

BY

KENNETH K. GOWEN

Library of Congress Catalog Card Number 2001133013

ISBN 0-9663222-3-1

Printed by Sheridan Books, Ann Arbor, Michigan

Copy edited by D.J. Bennett
Interior Design and Cover by Kelley Sharp

Published by
KAY- DOT Publishing LLC
714 Manor Dr.
Oxford, Mississippi 38655
(662) 234-1970
email: gowen2@dixie-net.com

Also by Kenneth K. Gowen

GRANDDADDY, TELL US ABOUT THE WAR

To Dorothy, my other editor

A DAY IN NOVEMBER

ONE

The cold rain was steadily dripping from the barren tree Betty stood beneath. The continuous thump, thump on her umbrella echoed the drumming in her head as she gazed at the rows of tombstones in the tree studded cemetery. She tilted her umbrella slightly trying to see around a dark figure between she and the grave, sending the icy rain down her neck. A cold chill enveloped her entire body. The day was cloudy, cold, wet, and dark. Such a miserable winter day was altogether appropriate for this occasion, rendering it even more depressing for Betty. The entire episode of the past few days became such a blur she was oblivious of her surroundings other than it was **a day in November.**

The Chaplain had spoken his last words. The rifle squad was preparing to fire a salute over the grave of Tony De Angelo - the man she had loved more than any other man she had ever known. Now, he was gone. The entire lifetime she had hoped to spend with him had vanished. Who was to blame? Could it be laid at the feet of the Chicago police, the pressure tactics of the OSS or could she bear some of the blame?

Would it have been better to have deserted the OSS and gone away with Tony while they were in Memphis? She stood desolate in utter despair.

Feeling a firm pressure against her arm, Betty raised her umbrella to see who was standing by her side. It was Larry, Larry Roberts. Larry had been one of the recruiters that brought Tony into the OSS. Larry's eyes revealed sadness and hurt as he compassionately smiled in recognition and sympathy. Larry knew that Betty held him partly responsible for Tony's death. The rifle fire cracked over the silent gravesite, sending sharp reverberating echoes across Arlington Cemetery.

It was then that Betty tuned out the present and began revisiting the past. Her mind went back to the small café in Memphis, Tennessee where she met Tony while working as a waitress at the Bon Ton - a little café on Monroe Avenue. It seemed as though years had gone by, yet in reality it had only been a few short months. Most of that time had been filled with fear and despair since communicating with Tony had been impossible.

Finally the graveside services were concluded and one by one of those who had braved the rain drifted slowly away from the internment site. Larry offered to take Betty to dinner or to some place just to talk, but she declined. Larry looked as though he did not know what to say. With difficulty he managed a parting promise.
"If I can ever help you in any way Betty please don't hesitate to call on me - please!"

In an effort to be polite, "you know I will Larry thank you very much."

She had no intention of ever asking Larry for anything. Her desire now was for an assignment out of the country. It was important that she keep busy in an effort to forget the past. 'How in the world did I get into this mess in the first place? I suppose it was patriotism ... well, maybe.'

TWO

Betty Peterson was born March 11, 1921 in Memphis, Tennessee. She was the younger of two daughters in the family. She had attended Miss Hutchinson's School for Girls through the ninth grade. She persuaded her mother to let her enroll at Central High School as a sophomore.

Enrolling at Central High School in the fall of 1936 was one of the most exciting moments of her life. Her sophomore, junior and senior years had been rewarding and exciting, but had passed all too quickly. Betty had been very popular with all her classmates, especially the boys. She was nominated for every class office as she moved through the school years. She was voted most likely to succeed in her sophomore year; and the most liked. In her junior year she was runner-up in the Miss Central High contest, but won as Football Queen. She always made top grades, and in her senior year she officially became the Dream Girl of Central High. In her final year the students elected her Miss Central High almost unanimously. Also in her senior year, she collected seven boy friends that all wanted to go steady with her, and no less than three marriage proposals. She did not believe in going steady, which made her more popular with the male students since she was available to date many of them. How many times she had been to Fortune's Jungle Garden on Union Avenue, a favorite drive-in for most of the students at Central, as well as other schools. It was famous for its great food, but primarily because it was the favorite "necking" place in the city. Vines cascaded from the trees over and between the parked cars, with colored lights intertwined, making it difficult to see the occupants of other cars. Betty liked the boys, and what boy in his right mind, did not like Betty - she had it all.

Although beautiful and smart, Betty was a sensible girl and wanted a career in the medical field, possibly even neurosurgery. Her 3.9 grade point average ranked as one the highest in the senior class. She was looking forward to attending Vanderbilt University along with several of her classmates who planned to attend also, including three of the football players.

One of the football players was Carl Wade. Carl, captain of the football team, had escorted Betty across the field at Crump Stadium when she was Miss Central High. What a night that was. She and her court rode around the cinder track waving at the crowd of 20,000 thrilling to their accolades and applause. Not only was Betty excited that she was the reigning queen, there was also jubilation over the football game. Central 20, Southside High 0. Even coach Murrah was smiling that night. This was a night she would long remember.

THREE

Time had passed all too quickly, and before she could believe it, she was on her way to Vanderbilt University in Nashville, Tennessee. She was excited about not only being at Vanderbilt, but also being there with Carl. Of all the boys she had dated while at Central, Carl was the one she was especially fond of, and even fantasized that after graduation they just might be married.

While it was exhilarating to be in college, there had been one world-shaking event that caused those who were old enough to attend college to worry somewhat. September 1, 1939 had just passed and everyone was fearful of the United States becoming involved in the war that Germany had initiated by invading Poland.

Being a member of the freshman class at Vanderbilt University, and taking twelve hours, required most of her time. The courses were hard and living in a small dormitory room, with only one small desk to share with a roommate, made studying quite difficult most of the time. There was little time for social activities. Betty now agreed with mother about not joining a sorority. 'Mother knows best.'

Betty saw Carl on rare occasions, and some of the other kids from Central, but not ever for any length of time. They needed to have a get together to just talk. Carl was a starter on the Vanderbilt freshman football team and was crazy about football. There were rumors that he would start on the varsity next year as a sophomore.

One Sunday afternoon Carl and Betty met at the drug store across the street. Carl thought it was an accident, but Betty knew that Carl usually went to the store on Sunday afternoons and she made it a point to be there. Football season for the freshmen was completed for the year and Carl had more spare time.

"Carl", she cooed, "how good it is to see you. How have you been?"

"Oh just keeping busy - you know how it is."

It was rumored that Carl had been seen in the company of a cute blonde on several occasions. Betty would not admit to herself, or to anyone else, that she was terribly jealous. She wanted to turn Carl's head in her direction at his bidding not hers.

"Have you been home lately Carl?"

"No, not since school started and I'm really getting homesick."

With a far away look on her face. "I wish we could go back to Memphis one weekend and see everyone."

After a long pause Carl finally remarked.

"You know Betty, I have two tickets to the Ole Miss - Vandy game. It's being played in Memphis on

November 4. Why couldn't we catch the bus to Memphis, go to the game, then see the folks?"

"Do you really think we can?" Her blue eyes sparkling with excitement.

"Why not! We can ride the bus to Memphis. You can visit your folks and I'll visit mine, then we can have Saturday afternoon to ourselves and maybe go to a Vandy Alumni party Saturday night."

If Betty had written the script it couldn't have pleased her more. A weekend with Carl might get his mind off that blonde and get him back on track with me. A smile came across her face that caused Carl to ask.

"What's so amusing?"

"Nothing, nothing that you would believe."

Time passed slowly for Betty as she waited with anticipation for the trip to Memphis with Carl. Finally the magical weekend arrived. On Friday, the 3rd, she and Carl boarded the bus for Memphis. As the bus hummed long the highway, their conversation was primarily about the good old days at Central. By the time the bus reached Memphis, Betty felt that she and Carl had recaptured some of that old feeling.

The kick-off was set for 2 p.m. Saturday November 4th. Carl and Betty arrived early hoping to see many of their friends. Places for fans to assemble before the game were very limited. Maybe across the street, or at a hot dog stand, etc. As the stadium began to fill with excited fans, there were plenty of people from Vanderbilt and Memphis in the stands. Carl and Betty met some of their old classmates from Central and made plans to get together after the game. They discovered that some of their former classmates were attending various other schools, while some had stayed home and gone to work, and others had married.

"Betty, you might know", said Marge, "Virginia and Margaret are students at Ole Miss and they'll be pulling against us."

"Yes," said Betty, "I heard they were in school down there."

Carl asked, "What is Virginia majoring in?"

"Boys."

They all laughed in agreement.

The game was secondary for the girls. They talked most of the time and paid little attention to the activity on the field. For Carl it was different. He would no doubt be playing against Ole Miss the next year and he wanted to learn as much as he could about their team. Ole Miss prevailed in the game by a score of 14-7. Carl thought to himself, 'it will be different next year.'

It was decided by the girls that instead of going to a Vanderbilt party and getting tied down, they would go to the Skyway in the Peabody Hotel and have a party with only the twelve of them.

"What about reservations?" Asked Carl.

"Don't worry Carl, good old Harry has connections and will take care of everything."

The tables were not in the best location, but at least they had a place to sit. The Skyway was crowded, mainly with students from Ole Miss. The music was good and the dance floor packed, to say the least.

At some point during the night at the Skyway, Carl admitted to himself that he was in love with Betty. Betty sensed something had happened to Carl. When they danced he held her as though they would never part.

"Betty, you know we have a long way to go in school, but I never realized how much I cared for you until tonight."

There was a long pause.

"Betty will you go steady with me?"

"Oh, Carl you know I will!"

As they kissed in the middle of the dance floor in the Skyway, fireworks exploded for both of them. The band was playing "High On A Windy Hill.' It was a time that Betty would never forget. Perhaps the tune the band was playing was appropriate in more ways than one - high and windy. Perhaps that was how their love affair would be.

FOUR

As the months went by, Carl and Betty continued to see one another and the fire that was lit in the Skyway that night continued to burn. Carl made the varsity and was the second string halfback on the Vanderbilt football team. Carl was looking forward to the Homecoming Game with Ole Miss on November 2, 1940. He had taken a lot of ribbing from the Ole Miss fans the previous year and wanted to shut them up.

Also during the year the Selective Service Act (draft) was implemented, requiring men to register when they reached the age of 21. Carl and the sophomore class would not be old enough to register, but the war was on the minds of all the boys in college. 'Will I be allowed to finish college?' Was the most often asked question.

The war in Europe was going very badly for the Allies, and it was a common belief that unless America helped England, that nation would not survive.

The Vanderbilt campus was alive with excitement preparing for the big homecoming football game with the University of Mississippi. Carl would not get to start, but the coach promised him equal playing time at the halfback position.

The long awaited game time arrived and the throngs of Vandy fans were behind the team and had every confidence they would win. The game was mostly defense after Ole Miss scored a touchdown. Finally Vandy got a drive underway and moved to the Ole Miss 15 yard line. The coach yelled for Carl to go in. The play was a halfback run between the right guard and tackle. Carl got the ball, and with all the power he could muster, burst through the line and scored. Vandy kicked the extra point and led the game 7 to 6. Late in the game Ole Miss came back and scored to win the game, 13 to 7. It was a big disappointment for Carl and the Vandy Commodores, but there was always next year. However, Carl was not excited about next year. It was a possibility that he might not be a member of the team.

Carl and Betty completed their sophomore year with good grades. Betty had no thought but that Carl would attend Vanderbilt his junior year, but Carl had been thinking more and more about possibly joining the Army Air Corps. Since he had two years of college he was eligible to enlist. He had been talking to some of the students that had already enlisted in the Air Corps who were very excited about it. This really set him off. He was ready to go. Carl, like many others, had been caught up in the excitement of an anticipated pilot's life. The continued coverage of the war in the newspapers, and on the radio - plus the movies - had done much to influence young men like Carl. Carl talked to Betty about his idea, but she was not in favor of such a drastic decision. Betty hoped that Carl would get over the adrenalin rush of such a rash move and go back to school in September.

Carl and Betty went back to Memphis for the summer and dated on a regular basis. When the subject of the Army Air Corps came into the conversation, it always ended in an argument.

"Betty, you are on my case, and I wish you would lighten up!"

"Carl, I don't want you to go into the service until you have to."

Such conversation would cover the subject that always ended the same way. Finally, September came around and it was decision time for Carl. He had made up his mind - it would be the Army Air Corps. Carl went to the recruiting office in Memphis and enlisted. Betty cried for half the night, but her tears would not change things. It wasn't the decision to join the Air Corps that brought tears, but the idea that Carl would no longer be around.

Betty went back to Vanderbilt in the fall of 1941 and Carl started his basic training in the Army. Their lives had settled into the routine, that their different life styles dictated until December 7, 1941. America was now in the Great War, and suddenly priorities were changed. What was important yesterday had little value today. Plans that had been made were put on hold making it difficult to plan anything for the future. All those of college age were plummeted into total shock not knowing what the next day would bring.

Betty went home for the Christmas holidays with the anticipation of seeing Carl. He was scheduled to get a furlough before going into flight training. They would have a few short days to share, then who knew what. They shared the fear that all young people faced - when would they see each other again?

Carl was scheduled to leave by train on the morning of December 23, 1941. Betty went with him to the Union Station to see him off. It was a sad time for them both - they were deeply in love. As they approached the gate that would separate them, Carl turned abruptly to Betty, looking deep into her eyes. "Betty, will you marry me?"

Betty had prayed that he would ask her to marry him, but for him to select this particular place and time took her completely by surprise. After catching her breath, she said in a shaky and broken voice.

"Darling, I will marry you and love you forever. You know nothing in this world would make me happier."

After a long embrace that drew most everyone's attention - - -

"Maybe after I get my commission I can get a furlough back to Memphis, and we can have a small wedding. You know I won't make much money, but maybe we can find a small apartment, or a room, to live in as long as I'm in the states."

"My dearest darling I don't care where we live or how much money you make, I will go with you to the ends of the earth."

As they stood before the gate that would separate them, it was time to finally say good-bye. Betty's tears flooded down her face as Carl kissed her.

"My you have such juicy kisses." They both laughed.

"Carl darling, will you write to me every day?"

" You know that I will honey."

"Promise me?"

"Yes, I promise."

Carl pushed away and forced himself to go beyond the gate. He would walk a few steps, then look back through the crowd to see if Betty was still there. Others were also saying good-bye, but it was not the same agonizing good-bye that Carl and Betty had to go through, they were sure. Betty was able to see Carl as he boarded the train, giving her a short wave as he disappeared from view. For a very long while Betty stood motionless. Why did she have such a hollow feeling of loneliness? After Carl had asked her to marry him, she should be bursting with happiness. Yet there was a strange feeling of foreboding she had never experienced before.

Betty and Carl corresponded regularly. Betty could hardly wait until the time came for Carl to graduate and receive both his commission and wings. She had planned the wedding so many times that it would be no problem when at last they could set a wedding date. As the winter gave way to spring, the surroundings changed. The flowers bloomed, but the pain of separation was not eased.

While sitting in class one afternoon, one of the instructors came into the classroom and gave Betty a note asking her to report to the dean's office. 'What in the world have I done', she asked herself. Dean

Astor's secretary ushered Betty into the Dean's office without hesitation. Betty knew that was not normal and she began to feel uneasy. 'Had something happened at home?'

Dean Astor was such a nice individual and a kind person. Betty had talked to him on several occasions.

"Betty," Dean Astor started his conversation as though he was trying to get the feel of what he wanted to say.

"Betty, Mrs. Wade called me from Memphis and asked me to talk with you."

A sudden cold chill engulfed her, for instinctively she knew that something was terribly wrong.

"Betty," Dean Astor started again.

"I am sorry, but Carl Wade was killed in a plane crash. Carl was such a fine man and ...."

Betty's head began to swim and she did not hear anything else Dean Astor was saying. She could not speak - only gasp.

"You must be mistaken, you must be mistaken." She murmured as she slumped into a chair.

Several days later in Memphis, at Carl's funeral, Betty had accepted the fact of Carl's death, and felt she had experienced her own death in the process. Life was over for her. Betty remained in Memphis with her parents for a week then it was decision time. Although devastated, she decided to return to Vanderbilt and continue her education. Maybe it was then that she made a promise to herself. She would never let herself get serious again with any other man.

FIVE

L arry Roberts and Betty had been classmates for three semesters. He too had a burning desire to be a neurosurgeon. Because of their common desires and goals, they had been thrown together in some of the same classes working on projects together. As a result they developed a mutual professional respect and comradeship toward one another. Larry was a couple of years older than Betty and had been in and out of school working at part time jobs to further his education.

Days had turned into weeks and weeks into months since Carl had died. For Betty time had little significance. Time was measured only by class and study time, not by the clock or calendar. There seemed to be no future for her, only the past. She had thrown herself into her studies and nothing else mattered. Finishing out her junior year, and maybe going to summer school, occupied her mind. The war was on everyone's mind. Several of the coeds at Vanderbilt had enlisted in the WAC's. Betty and Larry were trying to rush their day of graduation. However, there were other events going on in the war conscious

17

world that they were not aware of, which would ulti-mately change the direction of their lives.

In May of 1942 a new organization was in the process of being set up. It would be called the Office of Strategic Services (OSS). America was not prepared for a major war. Europe had been on the bubble between war and peace for years. Because of this, England, among some other countries, had moved ahead in the field of intelligence. The absence of an intelligence service was just one of the major road-blocks encountered by the leaders of America as they faced the reality of a major war in Europe. For months a fierce battle waged over the need for an intelligence agency; if, indeed, there was a need, what would be its function; in what area of the world would it operate, and who would be in charge of such an organization? The struggle would go from the President to those of lesser importance down the line and then back again. After weeks and months of this continued struggle for power and identity, the Office of Strategic Services (OSS) was created. It was restricted from operating in the continental United States, Canada, and Latin America.

It was also in early summer of 1942 that a man named Tony De Angelo was thinking seriously about moving to Memphis, Tennessee. How could such unrelated events affect the life of Betty Peterson? If you asked her - she would have answered without reservation - absolutely no way!

As Larry and Betty headed toward their senior year, the war was becoming more and more a part of

their lives than they would like to admit. Larry had already registered for the draft and felt that he might not finish his senior year before going into the service. "You know Betty, I believe this war is going to have to be settled before I can get serious about college. I just don't see any future as it stands right now."
Betty understood how he felt. He had become her confidante, protector and dearest friend. Larry was always around looking out for her as though she was his sister, and Betty enjoyed the attention. She had been so lonely since the death of Carl, and Larry was the one person who had been a true friend to her.

One afternoon, while hanging around in the campus store, Larry met a very nice man named Mr. Peterson. (No relation to Betty) A friend of Larry's in the ROTC introduced them. Larry thought little of the meeting. The conversation seemed trivial and there was no apparent reason for the two to ever meet again. However, the meeting was no accident. Mr. Peterson excused himself to use the telephone, cleverly removing Larry's water glass from the table without anyone noticing. (Larry's fingerprints were necessary) Larry was good looking, with a great smile, good eye contact and a great conversationalist. Mr. Peterson had been observing Larry for some time and had decided that he just might be a good candidate for the newly formed OSS. Larry was from mid-America; a farm ten miles west of Brownsville, Tennessee.

A week had passed when Mr. Peterson appeared again. This time Larry was sitting in the corner of the

Student Center building studying. Larry looked up and smiled in a polite manner expecting Mr. Peterson to pass on by, but he didn't. Mr. Peterson pulled up a chair, looked Larry straight in the eyes and said.

"Larry, would you like to take a ride with me?"

At first Larry did not know what to say or what he should do. While Larry was trying to read something into Mr. Peterson's face, Mr. Peterson began to stack Larry's books as though he knew Larry would accompany him. Finally Larry looked up.

"Sure Mr. Peterson, I'll go with you. Where to?"

It was a ride that changed the life of Larry Roberts. After driving a few miles from the school Mr. Peterson identified himself, and his mission.

"Larry I am from the Office of Strategic Services, in short, the OSS. This agency is vital to the interests of the United States. We have no intelligence gathering organization such as the British MI-6 or the Russian KGB. Men like you are desperately needed to staff the OSS. You could wait and be drafted and serve in the military and be just another soldier or sailor, or you could get into this vital part of the war that must be won."

"Would this mean that I would be a spy?"

"If you would like to call it that Larry, you may, but it is much more than just being a spy! It is a war that must be fought in the shadows before the major war can be won." Think it over Larry, take a couple of weeks if you would like."

As Mr. Peterson started to walk away, he turned sharply to face Larry.

"By the way Larry, the OSS can use smart, capable women. It would seem to me that you know such a person - you know, Miss Peterson."

"How did you?"

"Oh, we know a lot Larry. I'll be around the drug store tomorrow afternoon, and look forward to meeting Miss Peterson." Mr. Peterson took a couple of steps, then glancing back,

"Let me know Larry."

Larry could not wait until the next day to tell Betty. He flew over to the pay phone, put a nickel in, and dialed Betty's dorm. As usual the wrong person answered the phone, and he had to wait until Betty could be called. Finally she came to the phone.

"Betty, you've got to meet me at once. I have something very important to tell you!"

"Larry don't you know what time it is? I am ready for bed and you know that we are not supposed to be out of the dorm this late."

"Yeah, Yeah, I know all about that, but you know how to get out without being seen, so meet me at the double oaks as soon as you can."

After a long pause, Betty agreed.

"Give me fifteen minutes. Larry, this had better be good."

Larry watched Betty as she moved from tree to tree to join him.

"What in the world is wrong with you Larry?"

It did not take Larry but a short time to lay the whole situation out as Mr. Peterson had explained it to him.

"Mr. Peterson wants to recruit you for the OSS."

21

Betty never thought herself qualified for such work. But the recruiters saw her differently. Betty was very good looking and would turn the eyes of any male. Although she was extremely attractive and delicate looking, she was very capable of taking care of herself. She was the type person who would not run out of gas, nor have a flat tire without a spare and jack. Perhaps it was her looks that caught the eye of the recruiters, and not the self-reliant trait, but put them together and the OSS had the type of recruit they were looking for.

"Larry you know this must be a joke. I'm not in least bit interested in joining some outfit full of spies. You know that I am not going to leave school, and my career!"

Larry understood her feeling since he was going through the same frustrations.

"Betty, I can understand how you feel, but won't you let Mr. Peterson meet you?"

"What for? It would be a waste of his time as well as mine."

After a long pause, Betty looked at Larry's pleading face.

"Well, all right Larry, but I will not change my mind." The next day Mr. Peterson met Betty and they too went for a ride. Mr. Peterson came down hard on the patriotic angle as he made his plea.

"You know Betty, everyone will and must do their part to win this war. If they don't we could lose, and that would change our nation from a free nation to one of enslavement. There is, of course, no guarantee that the allies will win the war."

Mr. Peterson paused to read Betty's face - was he getting to her?

"We don't know if England will hold out long enough to give us a base of operation against Germany. They are taking a terrific beating right now."

Mr. Peterson was aware of Carl's death.

"You know we cannot afford to forget those who have already died and let their deaths be in vain."

Betty was visibly moved. After a long pause; "Mr. Peterson I will give it serious consideration." Betty knew she had been convinced. Now instead of she and Larry being neuro-surgeons, they would become international spies, parachuting into enemy countries and blowing up things.

SIX

It was July, 1942 when Betty Peterson and Larry Roberts were sworn into the Office of Strategic Services for the duration; for better or worse. They were sent to a training camp somewhere in Virginia. The camp would later be referred to as the "farm."

For Betty this new career was in some ways exciting, even though it required long hours of hard work. She and Larry were together most of the time during training. They both wished they could see a town with lights and good restaurants. The steady diet of GI food had long since turned them against food. To brighten their day, they could see a movie once a week, but it was always one that they had already seen in Nashville or Memphis.

As they entered the remaining days of their training, there was one big event that they dreaded in one way, but looked forward to with subdued excitement - the "jump." They knew that they would have to make a jump, but as luck would have it, they had to make two. The first would be made during the daytime and the second would be made at night. Neither Betty nor Larry had ever flown in a plane much less had to jump out of one. They were each given a main chute, and a pack chute, just in case the main chute did not open.

"Larry," Betty called with a shaky voice. "If the main chute doesn't open, I will never be able to pull the cord on the small chute. What am I going to do?

"Pray that you won't have to Betty."

They boarded the DC-3, and as the plane climbed to 3,000 feet, the Army Sergeant barked, "Hook-up!" Betty's hands were shaking so hard the sergeant had to snap the hook on the cable for her. She looked up at him, and said in a broken voice.

"I don't think I can jump out of that door."

"Don't worry, I'll push you out of the door, I have had to do that on other occasions."

Betty felt consoled that she would not be the first.

Larry, hearing the conversation, did not want it said that Betty could not make her jump, so he motioned to Betty to step up to the door first. After all she was a lady and should go first. The real reason was to walk her out of the door if she did not jump on her own.

Betty closed her eyes held her breath and jumped. The wind raced by her body as though she were in a wind tunnel. Then the terrific jolt when the parachute opened. She was then able to open her eyes and see the bottom of her white chute, then look down at the ground. "This is incredible", she said to herself - hanging by a strap looking down on the earth as though she were a soaring bird. 'Where is Larry, I can't see him. Did he jump? Did his chute open?' She was drifting down rather rapidly, and she now had to think about landing. She was told how to do it but would she remember. As the ground rushed up to greet her she again held her breath and closed her eyes as the earth gave her a rough reception. After rolling over a couple of times she was able to get to her feet and start pulling the chute to the ground. As she struggled with her chute she heard a voice from above.

"Hey Betty, look at me."

She looked up and there was Larry coming to the ground in his beautiful white umbrella. Betty removed her chute harness and ran to where Larry had landed. They both were laughing. There was a spontaneous hug as they both clung to each other a full minute. They were happy they had made the jump and thankful that it was successful.

Larry looked up in the sky, then at Betty.

"I'm ready to do that again."

"I am too. That was fun, and you didn't have to push me out."

Later when they made their required night jump the feeling was not as joyous. The best way to describe a night jump - it was nerve racking and scary.

There was a simple ceremony for the class when they finished their training. They were officially members of the OSS. October 21, 1942 marked a day they felt would never be forgotten. The class was granted a seven-day leave. Betty headed for Memphis and Larry went to his home near Brownsville, Tennessee.

For Betty and Larry being a part of the OSS was

A DAY IN NOVEMBER

perhaps the most important accomplishment of the year. They had no idea that the expected accomplishments would become larger and more difficult. While they had been in training an enormous operation that would span the Atlantic Ocean was being carefully planned. Such an operation would directly affect the lives of three people - nothing would ever be the same for them again.

SEVEN

The African campaign had been planned and was now in the process of being implemented. In time the African campaign would be concluded successfully leaving the German and Italian armies defeated. The next move would be to the continent of Europe. The British wanted the Mediterranean Sea safe for navigation so they were pushing for an invasion of Italy.

It was a deep concern for many who contemplated the invasion of Italy; such an operation would be costly. The possibility of an immediate victory was dimmed because of the difficult terrain that covered Italy. There were many rivers and mountains that were linked together by deep valleys. Roads in Italy were limited and in bad weather most would be of no use to an army on wheels. Such a campaign, even if the initial invasion were successful, would be costly in lives and could be a set back in the pride and confidence of any army. There was a formidable force in Italy. Both German and Italian divisions were numerous and well equipped. The Italian navy was a powerful force to be reckoned with if an invasion took place. The joint Axis force added up to a very difficult campaign. As it looked at this time the Axis forces would far outnumber any Allied army that could be put into Italy in the foreseeable future. The American High Command was not interested in any campaign, but the invasion of France, which would be across the channel from England. As so often was the case, there had to be some type of compromise worked out that would please everyone. It was believed by both sides that the key to success would be to get Italy out of the war.

A dictator had ruled Italy for many years. The people had become adjusted to responding to this type of leadership. If this leadership cannot function, the government ceases to function. Would the Fascist government of Italy collapse? Would the army and navy surrender? If this came about it would be the answer to a very difficult campaign. Most of the planners believed that this was a good possibility, given their understanding of the Italian government and its people. It was decided to try to implement such a plan. Who would do it? No one had the answer, but there were a couple of suggestions that had merit.

"Why not have the new OSS organization have a go at it, along with MI-6," suggested one British General.

"Let's let the OSS spearhead the operation, and be assisted by MI-6."

"Agreed."

The following questions were passed to the OSS. Could such an operation be carried out with a greater chance of succeeding than failing? If so, then how could such an operation be carried out? If the answer to the first question should be yes, then give them time to present a plan. A tentative date for the invasion of Italy could possibly be July, August or September. If July should be the date, then the mission would have to be carried out no later than early June. Therefore the OSS would have only until December 1942 to decide on the feasibility of the plan and begin to set it in motion. It was decided that January 1, 1943 would be "D" day for the complete plan to be approved by the high command.

As the OSS hashed and re-hashed the suggestion that the number one man in Italy be hit, there seemed to be more questions than answers. After hours of questions and answers it was the opinion of the OSS that, in fact, this could be done. Every available man was put on the project to come up with a workable plan. One day lengthened into another, then to another, until a painstaking plan was devised, but with one missing ingredient - a native Italian who was familiar with the lay of the land, and the people around the city of Rome. The Germans were not easily fooled. The Gestapo was a very sharp and intelligent organization. MI-6 had been feeding the young OSS organization with information on German intelligence and it was learning fast, but they needed more time to have agents that could be expected to carry out an inside job like this operation. It was concluded that it would be more suitable to recruit someone else for the job.

EIGHT

New York, Chicago, or Detroit would be the logical cities to seek out a prospective agent. The ideal candidate would be a man in his mid-twenties, who could speak the language fluently, with the proper dialect used around the Rome area; someone with a record - preferably with a couple of pending charges that could be used for pressure to persuade him to join the organization.

A review of the files in the Chicago Police Department found several prospects - among them was one Tony De Angelo. After an arduous review of the files by the OSS it was decided that Tony was their man. He came closer to the required credentials than any of the other prospects. There was no time to waste. However, one slight problem remained. They didn't exactly know where or how he could be located. After a diligent search it was determined that Tony worked at a club in the Chicago area. Two detectives were sent to the Diamond Club. After a check with the manager they were informed that Tony had recently left the club, and his closest associate was a colored boy named Amos.

"Where is Tony De Angelo boy?"

At first Amos did not know what to say. He was afraid Tony was in trouble and he didn't want to rat on him. Yet the police meant business.

"Where is Tony, boy?"

"Ah, he, he went down to Memphis, I think."

"You think!" yelled the big tough looking policeman.

"Listen boy, you had better know."

"Where in Memphis did he go, boy?"

"He went to work at a place I thinks they call da Bon Ton. It's a café in downtown Memphis."

"This had better be on the level boy, don't make us have to come back out here or you'll wish you were back in Africa, understand?"

"Ya suh, I am tellin' you da truth!"

A phone call to the Memphis Police Department was returned within four hours with the confirmation that Tony was indeed working at the Bon Ton. This information was in turn passed on to the OSS. Tony would have to be checked out to determine his loyalties. Could he be trusted as an American agent or would his loyalties be with his home country of Italy. Asking such a question meant nothing; such an answer could only come from someone that really knew his true feelings.

The most reliable method would be to have someone gain his confidence, and who was better suited for such a mission than one of the female agents. At the time all the experienced agents were on assignment. This presented a real problem. After some time had passed, and a lot of head scratching,

"Say, what about that new recruit that I saw up at the camp, you know that Betty Peterson," suggested Bob. "Yeah," chimed in Greg, "she's a real looker."
After moments of deep thought the section chief said, "go get her!"
A check in the front office revealed that Miss Peterson was on leave and was probably in Memphis.
"I don't care where she is or what she is doing, get her in here at once," snorted the chief.

Betty boarded an American Airlines plane out of the Municipal Airport in Memphis for the flight to Washington, DC, by way of Nashville and Lexington, Kentucky. During her flight she was trying to imagine why she had been called back to Washington before her leave was up. Could it have to do with the African campaign that was rumored to begin soon? Was she being dumped for some reason? She wondered.

When she arrived at her section chief's office, she was surprised to find that all of her guesswork was way off the mark. This was not going to be an exciting spy case, but a domestic exercise. She could not believe her ears.

"Go to Memphis and check out a waiter!' she blurted out.

"I know you don't think much of your first assignment, Betty, but it is up to you to determine this man's loyalty and if you are wrong in your assessment it could cost the lives of your fellow agents."
"But why me?"
"We must know for sure that this man can be depended on to do a very difficult job", continued the

chief.

Betty was still confused about her part in such a seemingly routine assignment, "you are asking me to tell you if this man - a felon - can be counted on to keep his word!"

"We know he is a felon, but there are felon's who can be trusted in the matter of patriotism."

The chief moved within twelve inches of Betty's face as though he was going to slug her.

"Loyalty, Betty, that is the question, not honesty. Is he loyal to Italy or to the United States, that is the real test and you must find out - and in a hurry."

With that the chief did a 180 and marched out of the room, leaving Betty with a bewildered look.

NINE

The magnitude of the great war had virtually shaken the lives of almost everyone between the ages of eighteen and thirty five. The war would make such an impact in every aspect of life, the life to which they were accustomed, would never return. Had there not been a World War II, the lives of Betty Peterson and Tony De Angelo would have never crossed. They were from two completely different worlds and by all accounts never should the twain have met. But they did, and nothing was ever the same for either.

Tony De Angelo was born in simple surroundings in the small town of Cisterna, Italy. Cisterna was one of the towns of importance between Rome and Naples. Highway 7 moved through the center of the town on its way to the Colli Laziali Hills and then to Rome. Cisterna would again be considered a very important, and much fought over town in World War II during the battle of the Anzio beachhead.

One of the many projects sponsored by the Mussolini government was draining the Pontine Marshes south of Rome. Cisterna was but one of the major towns in the effected area. Factories were to be built, swamps turned into useable farmland for cultivation, and after the project was completed it would then result in another great accomplishment for Mussolini. To drain the huge marshes, large drainage ditches the size of some small rivers had to be constructed, and, for obvious reasons, it was named the Mussolini Canal. The entire town of Aprilia (The factory) was built as a show place. There were other towns in the area such as Littoria, Anzio, and Netunno, to name a few. The port cities of Anzio and Netunno were resort areas where the wealthy in Rome went to the beaches on holiday.

Although Tony was growing up in difficult times, he did have an opportunity to earn money as a 'water boy' working for the government on the various projects in and around his hometown. His father had a steady job working as a ditch digger, dirt mover, or whatever he was told to do. At least he was making enough money that his family did not go hungry. Tony was the oldest child in a family that numbered ten. Two of the children had died as infants and the oldest daughter had run away with a soldier and was thought to be in the Naples area.

Those fortunate enough to have a job working for the government felt somewhat secure, yet, it was becoming clear that Mussolini, a dictator, was leading Italy into wars of aggression. This was of great concern to the thinking Italian.

The De Angelo's had relatives in America. There had been ongoing correspondence between America and Italy regarding Tony's family moving to America. It would be a difficult decision to make, but when common sense thinking was applied, there was no reason for them not to move to America. Every liare that could be saved was put aside to cover the expense of such a move. The relatives in America would help also. As they made various applications to leave Italy, Tony's age was changed to fifteen so that it would not look as though they were leaving to keep Tony out of the military.

The De Angelo family arrived in New York, NY, Ellis Island, September 1933. Tony was actually seventeen when the family moved into the Italian section of New York among relatives. Their meager housing consisted of one main room, and a small kitchen with running water and a sink. The family managed to purchase two beds from a salvage company for $5.00, which included the springs. The small children slept on floor pallets.

As the family settled in, the father landed a job at one of the laundry/cleaning plants in the neighborhood. The pay was $12.00 for a six-day workweek. At seventeen Tony was expected to have a full time job, but he was not about to become a slave to some two-bit job like his father. He was going to make money the easy way. It was not long before he made contact with a man at the pool hall that they called "Big Al." He flashed plenty of money and drove a Pierce Arrow car. Tony let Big Al know up front that he was interested in making some easy money, and whatever method used was not a problem. Al looked at the kid, pulled his cigar out of his mouth and growled.

"Get lost boy, this is a man's world!"

"I just thought I would ask," Tony said with a whipped look on his face. Tony did not give up even though buffeted by the sharp remarks of Big Al. He knew that this man had the "big bills" and Tony wanted a share.

Finally, after hanging around the pool hall racking balls, and holding coats, the break finally came.

"Kid," bellowed Big Al, "come here."

Tony could hardly believe his ears. He almost ran across the room - remembering the large roll of bills Big Al carried in his pocket.

"How would you like a job?"

"Would it pay much Mr. Al?"

"It will pay much more than you are making now, which is about nothing," snarled Big Al.

"All you have to do boy is deliver a few sacks to several locations around the neighborhood, and if you do this without messing up, I will pay you $.50 for each sack you deliver. You could make two or three dollars a day."

Tony could hardly believe it; 'why that'll be more than my papa's makin' working six days a week. I could make that much without workin' all day.' he told himself. With a big grin on his face, Tony looked at Big Al like he was Santa Claus. "I'll be glad to take the job Mr. Al. When do I start?"

"You'll start in the morning by meeting me at the back of the old garage down at 57th and Newberry," said Big Al as he bit the end of a new cigar.

Tony arrived early the next morning at the appointed location. After waiting for fifteen minutes or so, Big Al arrived with six sacks in his arms for Tony to deliver. Each sack was tied with a string and Tony was not to open any of them.

"You just deliver one sack to each address on this list. Knock twice on the door and place the sack at the bottom of the door and leave. Got it?"

"Yes sir, Mr. Al, I got it!"

Tony thought the sacks were awfully heavy to be so small, and wondered what was in them. He followed instructions to the letter and made his delivery without a hitch. Big Al was waiting in the pool hall for Tony to return.

"Are you sure you made the deliveries without a hitch kid?" Asked Big Al with a bit of skepticism in his voice.

"Sure I did Mr. Al - without a hitch."

"Okay boy, here is your $3.00."

Tony could hardly believe his eyes.

This was just the beginning. It was not long before Tony had a delivery route with twelve addresses, jumping to six dollars a day. By now Tony knew what he was delivering and also knew that it was illegal. The problem he now faced was what to do with the money. To spend the money the way he would like to would bring on questions from his parents. If he couldn't spend it, what good would it do him? Maybe he could purchase a few things and keep them down at the pool hall.

First Tony went to the pawnshop and bought a

.38 caliber S&W nickel plated pistol. It would shoot six times and had a two-inch barrel. It was just the right size to hide under your coat. Everyone had a rod, but Big Al had two. He then bought a new pair of shoes and a sport coat with contrasting striped slacks. Tony could not take his flashy clothes home so he decided to keep them, along with the shoes, down at the old garage and change each day so that he would look prosperous as he made his rounds. Maybe if he hid his prosperity his parents might not get wise and start asking questions.

As the deliveries continued to increase so did the money. Tony began to look for other ways to enjoy his big earnings. It didn't take long for someone to suggest he should bet on the horses.

"You know you could double or even triple your earnings from a couple of good races each day. That's the way we make our real dough Tony!"

'If that could happen it won't be long before I can drive a cad.' Tony thought. Although Tony played the horses and spent a lot of money, he never seemed to be able to win at the races. He did not catch on to the fact that the races had been run before he could bet on them.

Tony tried his luck at pool. Sometimes there would be games for as high as five dollars, but he mostly played for a dollar a game playing "eight" ball. Tony could never win at pool either. It seemed that he was losing more of his money than he was spending on himself. By now his father and mother had become suspicious. Tony seemed to have too many hobbies for someone who was unemployed. When confronted, he denied any wrongdoing.

One day while making a delivery, a drunk driver ran over the curb, hitting a fruit stand and knocking Tony and several other people to the sidewalk. During the accident one of Tony's delivery packages hit the concrete and its contents splashed on the sidewalk. The crash attracted the attention of a police car cruising the block. As the officers started checking those that might have been hurt in the accident, they quickly realized that the damaged goods was, none other than, booze.

Tony was taken to the station and asked a lot of questions. The police told Tony that he could be put in jail for a long time for selling bootleg whiskey. Tony started doing some powerful thinking. His alibi came naturally.

"I didn't know what I was delivering!" a frightened Tony blurted out. One of the policemen looked at him with eyes of steel.

"If you didn't know what you were delivering, can you tell us who asked you to deliver the bags?"

Now Tony was really in a corner. If he didn't give them a name, they would put him in jail for sure. If he gave them Big Al's name, that would be his end. Big Al would have him rubbed out. While the interrogation was in progress the police had called Tony's mother to come to the station. She went by Papa De Angelo's place of work and informed him of Tony's condition. Hours had gone by, but Tony had refused to answer any questions asked by the police. Finally

Tony's mother and father took Tony in a room offered by the police - that was bugged - to try to get him to talk.

"Tony, if you didn't know what was in the bags the police will believe you, only if you tell them who gave you the bags you were delivering," pleaded his mother.

Finally Tony broke down and gave the police the name - Big Al. The police knew who Big Al was and had been trying to get him on a charge of bootlegging, as well as several other violations. Now they had a live witness for the bootlegging charge. Big Al was arrested and put in jail to await his hearing. At the hearing the judge refused to set bail, so Big Al had to remain in jail until the judge heard his case in thirty days.

The De Angelo family had at least thirty days to make some critical decisions. If Big Al beat the charges Tony's days would be numbered. Sooner or later Big Al would get his revenge. And, the entire family might be at risk. If Tony were unavailable to testify, the police would not have a case. The family knew they had to leave New York with haste. It was decided, after talking to close friends - and among themselves - they would move to Chicago, Illinois. Chicago was a big city and they could probably blend in there without being noticed.

TEN

The move to Chicago was made with little effort. Two worn suitcases and a couple of boxes carried on the train were not difficult to transport. The family left behind a couple of bed-springs and a small chest of drawers. After settling in with their Chicago relatives, and arranging to sleep on the floor for a while, living in Chicago was just as simple as living in New York.

Finding jobs was not easy. There were people walking the streets and beggars were stationed on every corner. Tony's father got a job working in another laundry, because experienced laundry workers were in demand. Tony was no more inclined to get a job in Chicago than he was in New York.

Tony knew enough about big cities to know where the action was, and where proper contacts could be made - the pool hall. Tony met a couple of the locals who were in the know. It was rumored that the two were into pulling jobs, and selling the loot to pawn shops. Tony tried to get in with the group, but they would have nothing to do with a newcomer. It would be a wait and see situation before they would consider talking to Tony. He did not give up. Finally, one day as he watched a pool game, one of the men sidled up, bumping him on the arm.

"Would you like to go for a ride?"

At first Tony did not understand.

"What do you mean?"

"It might be worth your time."

"Sure, why not."

That was the beginning of Tony's business career in Chicago. The operation was simple. They would break into small businesses and take the loot - such as it was - to pawnshops, then split the take three ways. After several jobs, it was decided that they should take on more lucrative jobs and hit one of the larger jewelry stores in the area. The break-in went without a hitch. The jewelry was taken to several pawnshops before they were satisfied that they were getting the most for their merchandise. After the sale was made and the money was split, it was decided to lay low for a while. The last job would give them enough bread to live on easy street for a few weeks.

Unknown to the three thieves, the Chicago police had begun a search of all the pawnshops for the missing jewelry. The owner of one of the pawnshops agreed to cooperate with the police since the stolen jewelry was found in his shop. The shop owner gave the police a good description of the man who came into his shop with the stolen jewelry. The police had little difficulty finding Chino Gonzaga. He was no stranger to the police. Chino, under the pointing finger of the pawnshop owner, implicated Tony and the third member of the gang also.

Tony was picked up and brought in for booking. He had no money for a lawyer. The questioning police-man informed Tony if he turned state's evidence, and confessed his part in the crime, it might go light for him since this was his first offense. He might even get off with only 18 to 24 months in the state pen.

"Well, think it over while I go get a cup of coffee."

As Tony sat in the little room alone, it was obvious to him that he really had no choice. What could he do but take the offer of less time in the pen? His parents would not help him, and he would not ask for their assistance, after all he made the wrong choice, and there remained the nightmare of New York. If it was discovered that he had fled New York to avoid testify-ing, he would no doubt be sent back. In that case he knew he would never get back to Chicago. Eighteen months in the pen might be his saving grace from the wrath of Big Al. (Tony learned later that Big Al had been killed by a member of another gang, while wait-ing for his trial.) Tony was 22 when he got out of the big house and returned to Chicago. It was 1938 and times were hard in Chicago, as well as other parts of the country. Though times were tough and jobs were hard to find, Tony had decided that he would do any-thing that would keep him out of trouble with the law - he was going straight.

It was difficult for Tony to think about living with-out having everything he wanted. The situation he had in New York was his style and he did not want to give it up. He was not ready to work eight to ten hours a day just to make a so-called "honest living." Yet he had been on the losing end of the high life and he did not like the consequences.

Around Chicago there were clubs everywhere. He knew this was where you could find people with money. It was the people that patronized these clubs that Tony needed to make contacts with. They would be his best chance for a successful future. He began to make the rounds of the various clubs in the Chicago area, but he did not know anyone of importance - no pull. All he was offered was a job as a busboy or dishwasher. There would be no way to make contact with the people of class in such a job. Tony had two choices; honest work or back to pulling jobs. There was something about working in a club that was more appealing than looking over his shoulder after each heist until he eventually got caught. He decided to don a dirty apron and head for the kitchen.

The Diamond Club was not the largest club in Chicago, but it did attract some of the best known of the rich and famous - so he was told. It was while working in the kitchen of the Diamond Club that he met and made friends with Amos, a colored boy from Memphis, Tennessee. Amos talked very little about himself and his hometown. He had lived off McLemore Street in south Memphis all his life. He knew a lot about Memphis.

Memphis was a city of some 180,000 people in the middle thirties. It was located along the mighty Mississippi River where cotton was king. The city was the transportation hub of southern mid-America.

Highways and railways crossed the city, supplementing the river traffic from St. Louis to the north, and New Orleans to the south. Many referred to Memphis as the home of big Ed, a political figure with powerful influence. It was said that big Ed wanted Memphis to be a family town, therefore no liquor would be allowed in the city. The city was dry, but there were places in the county where booze was plentiful.

From a radius of 150 miles around Memphis, people frequently visited the city on business or pleasure and sometime both. There were several fine hotels, but the number one hotel was the Peabody. Large department stores were located on Main Street, along with first run movie theatres and drug stores. Restaurants were as plentiful as gas stations. Downtown Memphis had something for everyone. After shopping, or taking care of business during the day, many were drawn to the clubs for the nightlife they afforded. The downtown hotels booked the big bands excellent for dancing - usually until 1:00 a.m. If this was not their pleasure, then there was the Silver Shoe, a club located twenty five miles to the east of the city.

The club had almost any kind of entertainment the delta "blue bloods" could desire. The Silver Shoe had a far-reaching reputation as one of the brightest spots for excitement and entertainment, comparable to Chicago, New York, or St. Louis. The club was anything but dry, although in a dry county. Of course there were the games in the back room and pretty girls.

Rumor had it that some of the "big boys" from up Chicago way had more than a casual interest in the club. Always at the door were two men who looked like they had just fought through the south side of Chicago. Everyone packed a rod and some carried two. No stick-up men would make a living around this club. In the back room there were the "wheels", "boards", and the "tables." Only at this club could one find such entertainment. The rich folks from Memphis and the surrounding area kept the back room busy. If the delta cotton men could not be satisfied at the Peabody, there was always room for them at the Silver Shoe.

During the summer of 1939 the most exciting event at the club had been the theft of the "big man's" Cadillac. One of the colored boys stole his car and headed for a drive into town. He had been assigned the job of washing and waxing the Cadillac. Having never been inside such a beautiful car, he had an overwhelming desire to drive it just a little way down the road. What would his friends think when they saw him in such a big car. Amos was able to fight the temptation until he started wiping the dashboard and steering wheel. All the shiny gauges and the feel of the driver's seat, was just too much. After looking around to see if anyone was watching, he was satisfied that he could drive off without being seen. He would be back before anyone noticed - he thought.

After a jerky, jumpy start he finally got the big "Cad" rolling down the road. One look at the gas gauge showed plenty of gas, as he cruised toward the

big city. He could hardly wait to see his neighborhood. In the excitement he missed the turn at
Bellevue and McLemore and before he knew it he was
on Highway 51 headed for Mississippi. Amos thought
about turning back, but maybe he didn't want to go
back. Now he was running - the faster he could get
away from Memphis the better.

Highway 51 was the main link between Memphis
and New Orleans. Amos went through towns like
Hernando not knowing just how far he had traveled
into Mississippi. At Senatobia he wanted to stop, but
he knew people would be wondering how he could be
driving such a big car. Finally the big "Cad" came to
a chugging stop. The gas gauge had dropped to
empty. Amos looked in every direction, but didn't see
a sign of a gas station. Up ahead he did see a small
sign along the highway - Enid, 1 Mile West. He
thought surely there must be a gas station there.

Amos began the journey by foot into the small
town, and as he walked around a sudden turn in the
road the first thing he saw was a gas pump on the
front of a small building. He had no money, but he
did have a plan.

"Mister, I done run out of gas and my boss is waitin'
in da car for me to bring some gas back. If you'll let
me have a gas can wit three gallons in it we'll sho
come back and fill up da car and pay you for da gas."

"What kind of a car are you driving?" asked the attendant.

"A black cad," replied the boy.

If one can drive that kind of a car, there is no reason

why he can't pay for the gas and my trip out there, thought the attendant.

"Come on boy, I'll take you back to your car."

"Ah, naw sir, I don't want you to do dat, I don't mind carryin' de gas to de car."

Instead of a three gallon can the attendant filled a five gallon can with gas and headed for the stalled car. Sure enough there was a new black Cadillac sitting along the road, but no one was inside. He looked at the colored boy. Amos started shuffling his feet and looking down at the ground. There is something wrong thought the attendant. No Negro dressed like he was would own a brand new Cadillac. The attendant was extremely suspicious by now. He quickly moved around to the driver's side of the car to keep the boy from getting into the car.

"How about my money for the gas?"

Amos looked down at the ground, shuffling his feet again.

"I, I, thunk I musta lost my money."

"Well, I will have to have something for making the trip and to pay for the gas. What have you here in the locker?" While asking the question he was opening the locker. To his surprise he found an almost new .45 caliber semi-automatic pistol. It surprised Amos as much as it did the attendant. With the attendant holding the pistol, and Amos unable to answer, he finally admitted stealing the car.

"Where did you steal this car?

"I, I done stole it off a da street in Memphis"

"Now, you know that isn't true, you had to have a key

to move this car. You had better tell the truth, because you're in bad enough trouble already."

"It's, it's the big man's car at the Silver Shoe."

"What!" Exclaimed the attendant.

"You're telling me that you stole this car from him!"

"Ya sur, I did steal dis car from him. But if you take me back they'll kill me."

After a telephone call to the Silver Shoe, it was decided to take the car and Amos back to the Silver Shoe the next morning. The town Marshall and the attendant made the trip to the Silver Shoe without a hitch. The "big man" appreciated the effort made in returning his car in excellent condition as well as the pistol. For his appreciation he gave the attendant $50.00, and a free meal for both men, and a return ride to Enid. No mention was made as to the colored boy's future.

ELEVEN

As the weeks passed, Tony and Amos became better acquainted and Amos was not as guarded in his conversations with Tony as he had been. As they rested between chores, Amos would always mention Memphis and refer to something he thought to be exciting about the city. Tony's end of the conversations always wound up on a negative note.

"I'm never going to get where I want to be working in this kind of joint."

This in turn would prompt Amos to say.

"Nothin's bad as dis in Memphis. Ther's the Peabody, the Silver Shoe, da Claridge and lots more of dem places."

Tony had heard from other sources about the possibilities at the Silver Shoe. It was one of a kind in the Memphis area and drew the kind of people he wanted to be associated with. There was one thing that really bothered Tony. If Memphis was such a good place, why did Amos leave? He had offered Amos several opportunities to tell him why he was living in Chicago instead of Memphis, but he always changed the subject. If Tony was to make a move to Memphis that was the one question Amos would eventually have to answer.

One day while they were resting out back with no one around, Tony decided this was his opportunity to find out just why Amos left Memphis.

"Amos, I've got to know something."

"Just ax me Tony an I'll tell ya."

Tony looked Amos straight in the eyes.

"Why did you leave Memphis?"

Amos looked surprised at the question. He looked down at the floor, then up to the ceiling, shuffling his feet, then blurted - "Dey ran me outa town. I stole the "big man's" car. Dey whooped me and told me to never be seen in dis part of de country agin."

After a long pause - Amos seemed to be regaining his composure. "I caught de Greyhound and com to Chicago to live width my brodder."

That was not the answer Tony expected, but he was convinced it was an honest one.

Tony would wait until spring, he would then make up his mind whether to move to Memphis or remain in Chicago. The winter was extremely cold in Chicago, and it was best all around to stay put until the ice and snow had melted. While the time went by slowly, Tony saved all the money he could. In the meantime he talked to Amos as much as possible about Memphis. Memphis was not as large as Chicago, but it might be better in that it had fewer clubs.

Finally the day came for Tony to make his move. It was difficult to leave Amos, for he had been a good friend, but for Amos it was emotional, he had never had a friend like Tony. As they waited for a cab, Tony turned to Amos.

"Don't forget to come to Memphis and visit me, they won't know when you're in town."

Amos never said a word. He just stared at the street and shuffled his feet. Tony shook his hand, put his bags in the cab and headed for the train station. Arriving at Central Station he picked up his ticket and headed for the gate that would allow him to board the Panama Limited of the Illinois Central Railroad for the overnight trip to Memphis.

TWELVE

On the morning of April 12, 1942 Tony stepped off the train at Central Station in Memphis, Tennessee. He went to the Adler Hotel nearby. It was an inexpensive hotel on South Main Street. There was not enough cash on hand to live in a hotel for very long so it was urgent that he land a job quickly. The first place he planned to apply was the Silver Shoe. He made a phone call to the club for a possible opening. Someone told him that the boss would be in the office around two that afternoon, but the only opening they had was for a bouncer.

"Have you any experience in this field?" Inquired a dry unemotional voice on the other end of the line.

"Well, I did work at the Diamond Club in Chicago." Tony neglected to say what he had been doing.

"Maybe you should come out this afternoon and talk to the boss."

"Fine, I'll be there."

Tony did not get to see the boss although he arrived well before his 2 p.m. appointment. The secretary went into the big office and returned, almost in one motion.

"You are not big enough to be a bouncer, and we have no other jobs available."

"I thought I would at least get to talk to the boss," said a dejected Tony.

"It's not necessary. The boss looked at you through the window and decided you would not do."

No need to debate the issue now. Maybe he had made some favorable impressions that might get him a job later.

Tony made the rounds of the places Amos had suggested, trying to find what he thought he could best qualify for - a waiter's job. The picture painted by Amos was maybe a bit too optimistic. Tony had no luck getting hired at any of the places suggested by Amos. Now he would have to try to get some type of job to fill in until one of the better places had an opening.

Walking the main streets of downtown Memphis had not been any more productive than the special places he had visited. Tony decided to hit the secondary streets. As he walked along he spotted a sign in the window of a small café - Help Wanted. It was the Bon Ton Café located on Monroe Avenue near a couple of bus stations. The job didn't pay much but it would provide enough to live on until he could find something better. He needed a place to room and board, but didn't know his way around yet. To his good fortune one of the waitresses at the Bon Ton told him about a place on Peabody Avenue.

The military draft had been in effect since July 1940. Most single men, 21 years of age or older, were either in the service or had been classified 1-A. Since the draft was on the mind of every male and most of the females, it was not unusual for Tony to be asked the same old question.

"When are you going into the armed forces?" Tony knew that he could not go into the service because he was a felon. By now he had a standard answer, and an excuse.

"As soon as my back injury is healed then I am going to volunteer." He would explain further. "I hurt my back while helping to move furniture from a burning apartment in Chicago."

Tony had been struggling with his job at the Bon Ton for several months. He had about decided to head back to Chicago. It seemed as though he had been in Memphis for years although he had only been in the city since April.

One day in early December, which had started off like any other day, in fact, turned out to be anything but. Without warning to anyone a gorgeous blonde walked into the Bon Ton off the street asking about a job. All the male employees were stunned and the females hostile.

"Could this creature be for real?" Asked someone. Her long blonde hair (Veronica Lake style), her crystal blue eyes, and that smile - what a smile. She stood in the middle of the floor up front as though she wanted everyone to get a good look before she made her move. Looking at the man behind the cash register, she politely asked,

"Could you tell me where I can find the boss?"

After a short pause; "I need a job."

"I am the boss," said Antonio. "Do you have any experience working as a waitress?"

She looked at Antonio, gave him a million dollar smile and said, "some."

As far as the male employees were concerned she was hired when she walked into the café. Antonio felt the same way, but he had to make it look official.

"The job doesn't pay much, and the tips are not that good."

"I just need a job. My mother is in the hospital - we're from Missouri, and I need to make some money so that I can live down here and take care of her."

"By the way, what is your name?"

"My name is Betty Peterson, Mr. Antonio."

"Forget the mister stuff. When do you want to start working?"

"I need a few days to find a place to live. I have been staying with a girlfriend. Since this is Thursday, how about starting on Monday?"

"Fine," he said with a silly grin on his face.

While all the male employees and even some of the customers were expressing their overwhelming fondness of Betty, Tony had been taking it all in but saying nothing.

"What's the matter Tony, don't you have eyes?"

Tony responded with a disgusted look. "She is just a conceited broad!"

Betty returned to her apartment on Belvedere, and made a call to Washington, DC. She was all set. No one seemed to be suspicious at the restaurant.

The OSS had gotten her this apartment and there was no roommate. If someone pressed the issue, she would simply explain that her roommate had moved out. She made one observation to her supervisor in Washington.

"This Tony might be more difficult than we thought."

Betty, Tony, and all those working at the Bon Ton were very busy during the Christmas rush. Since the café was close to two bus stations, travelers gave them all the business they could handle. In addition, there was the Wm. R. Moore Dry Goods Company and several other businesses in the same area that kept them busy at noontime.

The café closed at 6 p.m. on Christmas Eve so the employees could attend the Christmas party Antonio was having for them. By now Betty had started to bother Tony. She was no longer a "broad", but someone he wanted to know better. There was a juke box (record player) in the café and for some unknown reason both Betty and Tony had the same favorite record - Elmer's Tune. A few of those present danced on the small floor at the rear of the restaurant. Tony wanted to dance with Betty but could not muster the courage to ask her.

Betty felt closer to Tony than anyone else. She had thought about the possibility of going out with him, but that was out of the question. She was not here to get involved, but to get information. Yet how could she really know him unless they went out together?

As the Christmas party wound down, Tony finally

got up enough nerve to ask Betty the big question.

"Betty, could I take you home?"

"No Tony, I have a ride home. Thanks just the same."

On yet another occasion Tony asked Betty to stay over and go to a movie with him at the Warner. Why the Warner? It was one of those Robert Taylor movies with a lot of romance. Again she turned him down.

As the cold days of January 1943 settled over the bluff city, the nights became very long and the days were bone chilling cold. Tony became very depressed that nothing he could do was making any points with Betty. This rejection was very painful for Tony. Working at his present job was getting him no place. He had long given up on the possibility of getting on at the Silver Shoe.

Betty realized that Tony was very unhappy and she knew why.

One day Tony announced to Antonio.

"I am going back to Chicago. I've had enough of Memphis and all the people living here."

Betty was in shock. If Tony went back to Chicago she could not finish her assignment. She felt it was because of her that Tony was leaving. Maybe if she relented and gave Tony a casual date once in a while he would change his mind and stay in Memphis. How could she change her behavior from unfriendly to friendly in a short time and make it seem sincere. He might get suspicious. There had to be a plan, but she had none. As she lay in her bed that night, Betty racked her brain to come up with a plan that would work.

She went to work the next morning with a tale about being followed from the bus stop to her house by a man that tried to force his intentions on her by making her walk with him. She went on to express her feelings to the other girls in the café, by saying she had been frightened out of her wits.

"I have never been so scared in my life. I don't know what I am going to do. How can I go home tonight alone?"

She knew that Tony heard every word, and if he took the bait, without prompting, the plan had worked; but what if he didn't?

She waited all day for Tony to react. Finally it was time for them to leave the café. Tony eased up by her as she put her coat on.

"Betty, I will be glad to see that you get home safely if you'll let me?"

"Oh Tony, will you?" Her blue eyes sparkling and her million dollar smile turned on to the limit. (If a man wanted to force his way on any woman in Memphis it had better not be Betty. She packed a .38 S&W Special in her handbag and it would be the last woman such a man would try to molest.) She played the part of a helpless female to a "T".

Betty began a program of "light dates", as she called them, with Tony. The idea of Tony going back to Chicago was never mentioned, at least in the beginning. While Betty was satisfied with light dates Tony wasn't. He wanted to go much farther than holding hands at the movies. He wanted Betty to agree to go steady with him - and a little more than a good night kiss at the door.

"Betty I don't know if you care about me or if you're just using me for your amusement."

"You know Tony that I like you a lot but I just don't want to go steady. (She knew she was not being truthful, because she was head over heals in love with this guy, but she had a job to do.) This kind of conversation went back and forth for weeks, getting Tony nowhere with Betty. Betty was fighting hard to keep her relationship on a business and friendly basis. It was not working for either of them. After weeks of this so-called light dating Tony made good on his threat, he left for Chicago.

Betty immediately phoned Washington to report Tony's sudden departure to Chicago. She was told to sit tight and not change her routine. They would be back in touch with her at the appropriate time. In the meantime the OSS had some work to do. A few calls from Washington to the police in Chicago located Tony and provided some interesting information on the past activities of Tony De Angelo.

Tony had gotten in touch with Amos as soon as he reached town. Tony stayed with his mother and father and tried to keep out of sight, but it was not long before some of his old friends knew about his return to Chicago. Word on the street was that the police were asking questions about how Tony was spending his time; did he have a job? The police had it leaked that they were about to make some arrests in regard to a robbery that Tony might have been involved in. Tony knew more than "might have been", he was in on that particular job.

Late one evening Amos appeared at the front door. He made the trip across town to tell Tony he had to get out of town as fast as he could. The police would likely pick him up the next day for questioning. Amos' visit upset Tony's mother.

"Tony, are you in some kind of trouble?"

"No Mom, they are just trying to get something on me."

"You know I taught you to be a good boy, and I don't want you to be bad Tony."

"I'm just going back to Memphis and get my old job back. I am not going to jail Mom. Don't worry about me. I'll write you when I get settled."

Tony's mother stood softly weeping. He loved his mother and was genuinely sorry for the trouble he had caused both his parents. Maybe he could make up to them some day for the embarrassment and disappointment he had been.

Tony took the advice of Amos and headed for the train station that night. The only place he knew to go was Memphis. He really wanted to go back because he could not get Betty out of his mind. Maybe he had been too demanding of her; perhaps she had changed her mind in his absence - at least that was a possibility.

Tony arrived at the Central Railroad Station in Memphis in mid-afternoon on a Saturday. He called the Bon Ton to see if Betty was working, but he was informed that this was her day off. Another call to her apartment found her at home.

"Hello Betty, this is Tony. How are you?"

There was a long pause on the other end.

"I'm fine Tony, how are you?" another pause.

"Where are you Tony?" Betty asked in a somewhat puzzled voice.

"Oh, I'm here in Memphis, and I want to see you tonight."

There was another long pause.

"Tony, I am sorry, but I can't see you tonight, I have a date."

Now there was a long pause on Tony's end of the line. Tony was boiling! 'How could she? Going out with someone else. I've only been out of town for a few weeks.' Tony's pride was on the line. Should he hang up, or give her an ear full, and then hang up?' Betty waited for Tony to say something. When there was no response, she said, in a quiet sweet voice.

"But I could see you this afternoon for a while if you wanted to come out."

Tony was in no hurry to give her an answer - still fuming. 'Who is this jerk she has a date with?' There was another long pause.

"Well I guess seeing you this afternoon is better than not seeing you at all." How could she be so cruel?

"You must understand Tony, had I known you would be in town and wanted to see me I would have been available, but I can't break a date this late"

"I understand what you're saying, but you could break a date if you really wanted to. After all I haven't been around for a while and you could make an exception." 'If she cared as much for me as I do her she would break a date with anyone.'

"You must understand Tony. Come on out this afternoon, I want to see you." She really sounded a though she meant it, Tony thought. He could hardly wait to see her.

"Okay Betty, I will be out in a little while."

Tony boarded the No. 2 Fairgrounds streetcar. As it rhythmically made its way down Madison toward his stop at Madison and Belvedere, he could hardly control his excitement. He wondered if Betty had changed, was she as pretty, was her hair the same? As he stepped off the car at Belvedere the butterflies in his stomach had taken over. He could not let Betty sense his excitement. He would play it cool and see if she would change her mind. It would mean a lot to him if she would break her date with this unknown jerk!

When Tony knocked on the door it opened immediately. Well, he thought that was a plus, at least she had been looking for him. When she swung the door open, she almost took his breath away - she was more beautiful than he had remembered. With her long hair cascading over half her face, her sparkling blue eyes, and that devastating smile, all the hostility Tony had been harboring vanished in the flick of an eye. He wanted to take her in his arms and never let her go; wanted to smother her with kisses and squeeze her to death, but he didn't. He was going to play it cool.

"How are you Tony?" Betty asked smiling.

"Oh, fine." Tony nonchalantly replied.

Betty turned and walked up the stairs to the sitting room. Her perfume left a desirable, tantalizing trail to follow. She looked like a million dollars in what looked like a new dress - at least it was new to him. As Tony walked up the stairs behind her, his jealousy was already melting down - he forgave her. After all, he reasoned, she could not sit at home and wait for him all the time. As he walked into the room he immediately spotted a large vase of fresh flowers on a table - obviously from a florist. 'Who is this jerk sending flowers to her? He's really out-doing me. I can't afford such gifts.' Betty had put them in a prominent place so they could be seen entering the room. 'What is she doing? Rubbing it in I guess. How could she?' Tony's blood began to boil again. If she was trying to make him jealous or mad she had succeeded. Now instead of wanting to smother her with kisses, he would much prefer to choke her - how could she? Their conversation remained on a friendly but cool basis. Tony tried once more to get Betty to break her date, but she would not budge.

"Well," Tony said as he got up from his chair. "There's no reason for me to hang around any longer. I don't want to hinder you from keeping your big date tonight."

"Now Tony, you wouldn't want me to break a date with you, would you?" 'At least,' Tony thought, 'I know how I stand. This guy rates with her more than I do.'

"Okay Betty, I guess I will be seeing you sometime

when you're not so busy. Maybe I could call ahead a couple of months, or so."

As Tony left Betty had no doubt about his feelings. If Betty was trying to make him jealous she had succeeded. Tony was more hurt than jealous. Maybe it was his ego. Playing second fiddle to anyone was not his style.

Tony thought, after he had left Betty's place, that perhaps he should have persuaded her to ride downtown on the promise that they would be back in plenty of time for her date, then after getting her there just not bring her back until he decided, which, of course, would be too late for another date. Maybe he should have taken her in his arms and begged her to go with him. Maybe he should have stayed at her place until she consented to go with him. But pride would not let him attempt any of these options. She must want to be with him or the date would be meaningless. As the No. 2 Fairgrounds streetcar neared the stop downtown, Tony had come to this conclusion. He would not give Betty up, but would let some time lapse before he would call her again. She had to suffer as he had.

Tony knew that he would be seeing Betty each day, for he had no choice but to return to the Bon Ton, he had to make a living. However he did not have to look at Betty, much less speak to her.

THIRTEEN

The entire affair between Betty and Tony had been an enormous setback for the OSS. To the OSS time was the primary factor, not romance. When Betty received a call from Washington it was not the call she had been expecting. Bluntly stated, the instructions were specific and to the point.

"You are well aware Flicker, that there is a time limit on this operation. Can you get the job done or shall we find someone else?"

"No sir," replied Betty. "I can, and I will, get the job done."

"Well," continued the abrupt voice on the other end of the line, "See that you do!"

Betty would have to lay aside both her personal feelings, and pride, if she was to get the job done.

'There isn't time for another fabricated imaginary man that followed her home scenario. Tony wouldn't fall for that kind of crisis again. There is only one way to handle this - just face the problem head on: bite the bullet and tell him how you really feel about him. No! I can't do that,' she thought. 'Well, tell him just some of the ways you feel. Tell him the guy I had a date with last Saturday is toast. Let me try that approach, and maybe that will clear up the problem of going steady - without committing myself.' By the end of the day her head was spinning, with still no clear resolution of the problem. As they were leaving for the day she watched Tony as he put his coat on and started out of the restaurant. It was now or never.

"Tony," waiting for him to turn around, "I am very sorry about last Saturday. You know you did leave town without even saying goodbye, much less telling me why you were leaving. I might have been mean, but it was only because I wanted to make you jealous. I wanted to know how you really felt about me."

"Gosh, Betty you know I'm crazy about you. I know I'm not in your class, but I'm hopelessly in love with you. I can hardly keep my hands off of you in the café.

"Well," said Betty, "we're not in the café now."

That was all the encouragement Tony needed. With one fell swoop he grabbed her up and put a clinch on her that almost broke her ribs, while at the same time planting kisses on her mouth that felt like a roaring fire on the front end of a train. All Betty could think was, 'well Mr. Peterson, you said to find out about Tony. I am finding out alright - it's like going over Niagara Falls in a barrel - there is no turning back.' Finally Tony released her, just so they could catch their breath, before the second round began. People walking up and down the sidewalk along Monroe Avenue were looking at them in surprise, as though they had never seen anything like this before. However, they all seemed to be in agreement with this particular street scene as they smiled and continued on their way. The middle of the walkway outside the restaurant was no place for this fanciful maneuver.

Without realizing it they had started to walk toward Main Street. The first movie theater they came to was the Warner; what movie was playing was purely incidental. They chose to sit in the cozy, darkness of the balcony. Tony squeezed Betty's hand, hugged her neck, kissed her on the cheek, then on the lips. Betty was shaken by this incredible experience; in total astonishment she wondered; 'what have I done? This has never happened to me before. What about my job, how can I analyze this man, or make any kind of a positive or negative report? I am head over heals in love with this felon!' She would be unable give an accurate report on Tony for the OSS, and furthermore, she did not want him in the OSS. He might get killed! Tony took her home around midnight.
Finally, after the tenth goodnight kiss, she was able to pull away from him and into her room. After a hot shower she crawled into bed, but sleep would not come. She tossed and turned for hours. At 2 a.m. she was awake; 4 a.m. was more of the same. Finally after several cigarettes, and endlessly tossing, it was 6 a.m., the night was gone without a wink of sleep. She waited until the office opened in Washington to make her call. When the operator answered, she asked for the number that would ring through to the office of

her immediate superior. While waiting she was over-come with guilt for failing to complete her first mis-sion, but during those waking hours she had to admit that she could no longer give an accurate and unbiased evaluation of Tony De Angelo.

Two days later while serving lunch at the Bon Ton, Larry Roberts and another agent, Vic Sarto, appeared at the counter and ordered two hot roast beef sandwiches, coffee, and apple pie. Betty had never met Vic, but she was well acquainted with Larry. From all appearances they were two new cus-tomers that had just hit town by way of the Trailways Bus Company. Before the meal was finished, Larry slipped a note to Betty instructing her to have Tony over to her place that night for a meeting with the two agents. Now was the time to bring the matter of recruiting Tony to a conclusion. Vic left a dollar tip.

It was not a problem for Betty to have Tony come over to her apartment at seven o'clock. He had been there every night since they made up. As Tony came into Betty's room he stopped short when he noticed the two men staring at him. He began to ask himself questions. 'Who are these men?' Immediately Tony had a feeling of foreboding. Immediately he supposed they were cops from Chicago. 'Have they found out something about me that will send me up?' (They were not cops, but they did have enough on Tony to send him up for about three years.)

Vic did not waste any time with Tony. He laid out their reason for being there that night in a very pro-fessional manner.

"Tony we want you in the OSS! Uncle Sam has a special job for you."

Tony's mind went into orbit. 'Who and why are these guys after me? How do they even know me?'

Suddenly it hit him; 'Betty' - his brain suddenly flashed hot. 'Betty was the go between, and this is why she's been in love with me lately. She was setting me up.' Tony shot an angry eye at Betty. She knew without a doubt what Tony was thinking. Tony's love suddenly turned to hate - yes, he hated her! Not only had Betty betrayed his confidence, she now knew about his past - his criminal record. Tony wished the floor would swallow him up. He had been used, ridiculed, and Betty had lied about loving him. 'What a sucker I've been.'

Agent Sarto brought Tony back to reality.

"You can join the OSS and serve your country or go back to Chicago and face possible charges on some unexplained activity in regard to several holdups and robberies in Chicago."

Tony flopped down in a chair, his heart pounding and his head whirling. He had felt so secure that his background was well hidden. Now his record was out in the open - he was just a jailbird - a loser! As he sat there with his head in his hands, his life, and the desire to live, had vanished; he was at the end of his rope. 'How could Betty do this to me? How can I ever face her or anyone else again?' A con, a loser, a no-good; everything went up like a puff of smoke. Tony had nothing to live for now that he had lost Betty.

Unknown to Tony, Betty was going through the

most intense suffering of her entire life. Her body was numb, her mouth dry as chalk, while at the same time she was choking back an oncoming flood of tears. To see Tony having to suffer at the hands of the OSS made her want to renounce the day she ever got into this cold blooded outfit. She could not bring herself to look at him any more.

After a long period of silence, Tony turned toward Vic with a look of utter hopelessness and gruffly asked,

"What am I suppose to do?"

"Well," said Vic, "you will have to go through a training period and then you will be assigned to a mission."

"A mission," exclaimed Tony. "What do you mean?"

Tony could not be told yet, but his secret mission had already been planned.

"We will be getting in touch with you Tony. Just stay put and maintain your normal schedule."

There was nothing left for him in Betty's apartment, he just wanted to get out of there as fast as he could and never come back. As Tony rushed out, slamming the door, Betty began to sob uncontrollably. She kept seeing the look Tony had shot across the room like a bullet that shattered her heart. She would never forget the hurt look in his eyes, or the anguish on his face.

After Betty had regained control of herself, Larry brought her a cold coke from her fridge, which she sipped slowly as she listened to Vic as he discussed the future plans for she and Tony. Tony would go to work as usual and so would she. In the next few days Tony would get a phone call from Chicago, saying his mother was seriously ill, and he should come home immediately. Tony's mother had been ill at other times, so the crew at the Bon Ton would not be surprised at this bad news. After arriving in Chicago, Vic and Larry would meet him there and take him on to the training camp.

As planned, a few days had passed when Tony received a phone call while at work. He left the Bon Ton for the last time. No one was the least bit suspicious. All of the employees were very sympathetic about Tony's problem.

Betty went home early that afternoon. Everyone thought it was because of Tony's mother. Betty was a basket case and one excuse was as good as another - she had to rest. She wondered if she had the toughness to keep doing the type of work required by the OSS. It was not in her plans to fall head over heals for Tony, or for that matter, anyone else. For her to have betrayed Tony as she did was unbelievable. How could she go on, knowing Tony hated her. She didn't blame him because he did not know the complete story, so therefore he did not understand. How could she make him understand that she still loved him no matter what. Betty made many attempts to write letters to Tony. They would begin ... My dearest darling ... Dearest darling ... I adore you . . .I love you with all my heart. On and on she would write, knowing that the letters would never be mailed.

Betty worked at the Bon Ton for a couple more

weeks after Tony's departure. As her reason for quitting, she said, "Tony has decided to stay in Chicago to be with his sick mother and wants me to come up there and get a job so we can be together."
Everyone around the Bon Ton thought she should go. After all weren't they madly in love?

Betty left the Bon Ton, and Memphis, but she did not go to Chicago. Instead, she flew directly to Washington and reported to her Section Chief to receive a new assignment, she hoped. They might kick her out after this last one. She didn't care about leaving the OSS under normal circumstances, but she did not want to be known as a failure.

FOURTEEN

Tony arrived at the training camp in Virginia where Betty and Larry had trained. He was instructed that he would not be allowed out of the camp for any reason while in training; a period of ten weeks. He had no idea what he was getting in to. Had he known he would have probably gone over the hill. The nights were short and the days were very long.

There were fifteen OSS recruits in the class with Tony. For the first couple of weeks they had to go through the same basic training as army recruits. This was an abbreviated training period, with the main emphasis on coordination and physical training.

After the basic training came the more specialized training. Much of their time was dedicated to learning various languages. German and Italian were the two emphasized. Tony had little trouble with Italian, but German was something new for him. There were some in the class that were up on German but needed help with Italian.

Some men from Fort Benning, Georgia conducted classes on parachute jumping. The first jump was a fright for everyone, but then there were the night jumps. These were nightmares. Several of the recruits just couldn't take the strain and were dropped from the training class.

After weeks of intensive training the class was split up into groups. Tony's group was comprised of six men. Their training was almost totally devoted to German and Italian language and mannerism. It was slanted in that direction so much so, that the group felt their service would either be in Germany or Italy. The mystery was not where they would go, but what would their mission be? No matter where they were assigned the group was ready. The training was more arduous than anything they could possibly face in the future - they thought.

One day after finishing a grueling run over the obstacle course, they were told to report to the orderly room.

"The following men will report to the main office at 0800 tomorrow. Rick Cardo, Tony De Angelo, and Joseph Golden. That's all."

They had the remainder of the day to speculate on what this was all about. Why these particular three men out of the group of six? Were they being kicked out?

Although they had been together for some time they had not been close, just to speak and pass a few words back and forth during a difficult time of classroom work. Since it was uncertain as to their future together, they would just let things remain as they were - somewhat distant for the time being.

Promptly at 07:50 the three appeared at the reception desk. As their names were recorded, they were shown to a room off to the left. As they entered the room they saw three chairs lined up in front of a large desk. The receptionist told them to be seated and that they could smoke if they wished. Thinking that they would be addressed quickly they sat at attention. After fifteen minutes it was apparent they would not get prompt attention, so they lit up a smoke and started talking. Of course the topic was - why are we here? They could only wonder.

After another fifteen or so minutes ticked away, a panel in one of the walls slid back and out of it stepped a rotund man. They noticed a large scar on his right cheek. He looked at each one of them, and motioned for them to move their chairs closer to the desk where he had taken a seat. As he shuffled papers on the desk they noticed a burned place on his right hand. For endless minutes in deafening silence, the man behind the desk gazed intently into each of the three faces before him, then spoke.

"Let me introduce myself; I am Mantis. As I call your name please nod in recognition. Tony De Angelo, Joseph Golden, and Rick Cardo. You three have been chosen for a very special mission." Another pause - for maybe some reaction from the team - then he continued.

"You will be moved to a another camp where you will receive specialized training as a team. The length of time for this training has not been determined as yet. It will depend mainly on how fast you progress."

He paused as though he expected some reaction from the group. He spoke in a low and somewhat indifferent tone of voice as he continued.

"You will learn to depend on each other, and will soon understand for one to survive, the group must make it happen. You will each be assigned a code name you will use as often as necessary."

"As long as you are here in training your team will be 2-X. You three men will be this team. Mr. Tony De Angelo of Chicago, IL will be known as Impala. Mr. Joseph Golden, from New York City, will be known as Kite. Mr. Rick Cardo, from Reading, Pennsylvania, will be known as Falcon."

This enormous man rose from his chair and stood looking intently at the group for a full minute, as though he were making sure he would recognize them in the future, then he asked,

"Are there any questions?"

Rick stood. "I have a question sir. What is our mission?"

He stared at Rick, then turned around and walked out of the room.

The secretary came into the room.

"Gentlemen will you follow me. Please return to your rooms and gather your personal items, clothing, and equipment. In about one hour you will be picked up and carried to your new quarters."

The new quarters proved to be a pleasant surprise. It was a self-contained small village. There were small roads, a house, a barn, the privy, (outdoor toilet) a couple of horses, a cow, and a small haystack.

All signs and markers were written in Italian or German. The small house consisted of the usual kitchen, washroom, bedroom, and sitting room. Off the kitchen there was a small stable where the cows could be milked on a cold or wet day. Every form of written material in the house was either Italian or German - even in the kitchen. All canned goods, packaged goods, boxes, cookbooks, etc., were printed in Italian.

The team was to live as though they were in Italy, they supposed. Their destination was no longer a mystery. The mission, however, was as much a secret to them as ever. There was no clue in this little setting as to what the mission would be.

At different intervals during their stay in the Italian village, they would be judged on how well they had adapted to their surroundings. Living under these conditions had to become natural - a normal way of life. One day Mantis and a couple of agents came out to view their living quarters. The two agents with Mantis spoke only Italian. They asked a lot of questions about the little farm.

"How often do you milk your cows?"

"What are you cooking for supper?"

"Have you seen any Germans?"

"Where is the privy?"

After the group left their little surroundings, they were seemingly satisfied.

"You know the big guy never said a word, he just gawked"

"Yea," said Rick. "I guess he never says anything

because it might take too much effort. He is a big man" They called him big because of his stature. He was 6'-6" at least, and must have weighed 290 pounds.

The team continued to attend classes on self-defense, close combat, explosives, communications and fire arms. It was vital that each member be an expert in each of these areas. But, as in most such groups, there would emerge one or two who would excel, and become the leader in a particular field. It was becoming clear that Rick (Falcon) was the demolition expert. Joseph (Kite) had mastered the radio. His ability to send and receive Morse code at the highest rate of speed made him the expert. He had to work with the base operators so that they would recognize his "hand."
Each operator has a peculiar touch unlike any other, and thus makes his key identifiable in enemy territory. There were times when such operators could be copied, but not often. Tony (Impala) seemed to have a better understanding of firearms. He could disassemble any German or Italian weapon and put it back together blind folded. But of course any one of the team could do all the jobs if it became necessary.

Meanwhile back in Washington:

Betty had been in Washington DC for some time and up to now had not been able to get a line on where Tony might be, even to know he was safe and well would satisfy, at least for the present.

She went down to her section chief's office believing she would be given an assignment of some sort.
She thought this would help get her mind off Tony.
While there she was invited to a dance the following
night. Although she had never liked Vic Sarto, since
the cruel incident with Tony, he had offered to pick
her up and escort her to the party. Since she had had
no other offers she agreed. Vic spiced up the party by
telling Betty there would be important agents at the
party and that she might find out something about
Tony and operation Alamo - the ultimate enticement.

The function was well attended. There was much
gaiety as couples danced and drinkers imbibed. Betty
sat at a large table with seven other people. Vic point-
ed out some of the well-known agents at the dance.
One man in particular, Vic suggested, just might
know something about Alamo.

"Can you introduce me to him Vic?"

"Sure, I'll get him over to our table, then you can do
the rest."

Some time later the man came by and spoke to Vic.
Vic stood and introduced him to everyone at the table
until circling around to Betty he announced gallant-
ly,

"And this is Miss Peterson." Betty winked at Vic as he
said, "Betty, this is Bob."

Bob spoke kindly, then strolled away to other tables
greeting people politely and chatting.

To Betty's surprise Bob returned to their table and
asked for a dance. He had already had too many
drinks, but at least he could stand and dance very

well for a fifty year old man.

"Are you married, Miss Peterson?"

Betty pulled back, looked him in the face with a knowing grin. "No, no, I am not, but I would like to be."

"I'm not married either. I used to be, but my wife left me and I am single again, and looking."

"You certainly won't have any trouble finding the woman you want. You are a very attractive man and besides you're a very good dancer." She said with a lilt.

"Do you really think so?"

"Vic tells me that you are a very important man in the OSS, and you have so much responsibility."

"Well, I do get around, if you know what I mean."

Betty felt she had Bob in a cooperative attitude.

"Tell me Bob, have you ever heard of an operation called Alamo?"

"Where did you get that name? That's supposed to be a top secret."

"Bob, I need some help. I might as well tell you the truth. I know about the operation and I have a very dear friend that I believe is a member of this team. I also have heard that they are somewhere in Virginia. It would mean so much to me if I could get in to see him."

"Oh, I might have known it! You would have someone on the string."

"Bob," Betty began, with the most pitiful look she could muster, then in a sugary tone asked, "would you help me?"

The music had stopped. Bob pulled Betty off to a corner of the large room where they could be alone.

"Betty I am not suppose to even know what I am about to say, but just for you I am going to tell you as much as I know. The team is in training at the OSS camp in Virginia. There are three men on the team and it is destined to go to Italy soon. The camp is restricted and unless you know someone at the top of the ladder it will be of no benefit for you to go there; you won't be admitted."

"Oh, thank you Bob. You are a real dear." Betty kissed him on the cheek.

She could not wait until she could talk to Vic. He had to get her out to the camp while Tony was still there. I know he is there. She kept repeating to herself.

The next day in the office Betty hit Vic with a big order.

"Vic, I know Tony is out there and I have got to see him. By what hook or crook can you arrange this for me?"

"Well, all I have to do is call the General - of the army - and request it!"

"Seriously Vic, how can I get out there?"

"Betty I don't want to get you excited about success, but I have one card that I can play. I know a driver that has been out to the camp on several occasions. He only goes there when he carries very important personnel. I will talk to him when he can be located and see what can be worked out. Give me a day or two."

"Oh Vic, that will be great, but do hurry."

Two days later:

Betty picked up her phone when it rang,
"Betty this is Vic. Meet me downstairs."
"Okay, be right down."
"I got the driver and he is willing to take us out to the camp, but there is one problem. He tells me there are three check points that might be difficult to get through. At times the guards recognize him at the first two checkpoints and just wave him through. The third and last checkpoint is at the camp and is much more thoroughly checked. Like a pass, or a visual I.D."
"If we can just get to the camp maybe I can find out something. Maybe I can bluff or charm my way into the camp."
"There is another possibility. We can get a forged pass; that might work. But, if we get caught we will be shot!"
"I don't care, it would be worth it if I could see and talk to Tony. You don't understand, I have got to tell him I'm sorry and beg his forgiveness before he leaves the country."
"Okay we'll make the trip late tomorrow afternoon."
The day was cloudy as the three occupants of a jeep headed out of Washington for the camp in Virginia. The beautiful hills and valleys of Virginia made the drive enjoyable, although quite long. Nearing the camp, they successfully passed the first checkpoint, then the second. They arrived at the main entrance only to be challenged by three MP's.

Betty decided to level with them and try to get their sympathy, but they would not budge. Without a pass, they could not go in. Betty tried to impress them with what she knew about the team hoping they would give in; they stood fast. As they talked back and forth, one of the MP's asked the Sergeant,

"Was that the group that moved out of the Italian village yesterday?"

The sergeant thought for a minute. "Yeah, I believe it was. I don't know what they were called, but there were three of them and they spoke Italian."

Betty knew that was the team. Her heart sank as she again had just missed seeing Tony, or at least leaving him a message.

As she looked at Vic, all her disappointment and sorrow washed over her face.

"Where do you suppose they have gone?"

"Betty there is no way to know."

It was a sad and lonely trip back to Washington. She came so close, but not close enough. Now Tony might be on his way overseas and she would never get to see him.

FIFTEEN

The ALAMO team had been moved into a hotel on the outskirts of Washington. There, they would undergo the final phase of their training. A team of professionals trained the team in the art of cloak and dagger. By living in an average environment, and experiencing the normal activities of a busy city, they would soon learn the complications of trying to follow someone, and in turn learn the difficulty of trying to keep from being followed. This training also included eating in the hotel dining room under European conditions.

"You hold your fork with your left hand not your right, etc."

After several days of this training, it was now time to think about the future.

"You men will be moved to another location in a few days."

They were restricted to their hotel room without a radio or newspapers. They had to hear, speak and read Italian only - positively no English in any form.

The team turned in around 9:30 pm. They were sleeping soundly when the door suddenly burst open, and the lights flicked on; then a gruff and unkindly voice barked,

"May I have your attention gentlemen? My name is Colonel Mayhew, formerly a member of General George Patton's staff, assigned to intelligence in North Africa.

Gentlemen your mission is top secret. You will not be told of your final destination, or your final assignment at this time. It is my purpose to fill you in on the general plans, and in particular your travel schedule. You will leave Washington on May 1st at 0300 hours. You will fly to Miami, Florida by way of Atlanta, Georgia. You will have a short stopover in Miami, then board a plane for North Africa, with another stopover at Ascension Island. You will probably land in Casablanca for a day or two then on to Oran where you will receive your final instructions on your objective. Since the African campaign is still in progress, circumstances will influence your exact travel plans. Are there any questions?"

"What about our clothes?"

"Good question. Take enough clothing to get to Miami where you will be issued lighter clothing. Any other questions? If not, may I say what has been said before - good luck!"

"We'll need all of the luck we can get," sighed Tony.

"By the way gentlemen, I will see you later when you get to Casablanca. The Colonel started out of the room, then turned and smiled.

"You may go back to sleep now until your next call."

"When will that be," asked Rick.

"At 0100,"

Now that the team members were alone and had time to digest the past few minutes, Rick commented,

"There is only one thing certain about this mission."

"What's that?" the other two asked in unison.

"We know absolutely nothing about it. Absolutely nothing!"

The night of April 30th was a short one. The Alamo team was up at 0100, dressed by 0130, and headed for the airport by 0145. Upon arriving at the airport with their luggage and personal items, they were escorted into a waiting room where they were told to strip.

"Wait a minute," exclaimed Tony, "I thought we were getting new clothes in Miami!"

"First you can't depend on what "they" say, and secondly - if you'll remember - you lose your identity in the OSS."

Then without any earthly goods, or a stitch on their bodies, they walked into another room where they were given new clothes, picked up a personal kit and boarded the plane.

"What about our personal stuff we left in the room?" asked a somewhat puzzled and bewildered Rick.

"You can claim those items when you get back." Chimed an unconcerned voice. Tony did not fret over his personal items, but he was crushed at the thought of leaving the small snapshot of Betty that he carried all the time.

The flight to Miami, with a stopover in Atlanta, required fourteen hours in the stormy weather that accompanied them. The trip was pretty boring for the team. There was nothing to occupy their minds except the past. By the time they arrived in Miami they were six hours behind schedule. A delay in Miami put them even further behind for their arrival time in Casablanca.

After a team of army personnel, and a group of civilians traveling with them arrived, loading of the plane began.

As the DC-6 taxied to the runway, a check of the team revealed one missing member - Joseph.
"Where is Joseph?"
"Search me, I thought he got on the plane behind me."
Rick rushed to the pilot's cabin and informed them that one of their team members was not on board. They took the place apart - no Joseph.

Finally a radio message was relayed from the tower that Joseph had become ill suddenly and would not be able to make the flight, but would come as soon as possible.
"Who gave you the message?"
"I don't know, it just came from the tower." Explained the pilot.
"We are cleared for take off, so I'll have to pull out or miss my place in line."
The plane roared down the runway and lifted into the air.
"I don't get it Rick, do you?"
"No I don't. You don't suppose he was kidnapped?"
Tony just shook his head, not answering.

It was dark when the team left Miami. There was nothing to do but sleep. After asking around, none of the passengers had ever heard of Ascension Island. Rick asked one of the flight crew,

"Where in the world is Ascension Island?"

The crewmember laughed and yelled back.

"It's in the middle of the Atlantic Ocean, if we can find it!"

"That's encouraging," yelled Rick. After endlessly droning through the night, the plane finally began to descend for a landing well after sunrise. The sun was bright, the sky was clear - a perfect day for a landing, on a spot no bigger than a postage stamp, in the middle of a huge body of water. Everyone crowded to a window to see Ascension Island. They enjoyed their four hour layover as they greedily drank piping hot coffee, and devoured fresh baked bread from one of the Air Force kitchens.

It was late afternoon when they were told to board the plane. Boarding with them was the same group of military officers that were on the flight from Miami. It seemed as though everyone was headed for Casablanca. Rick was curious about the civilians on the trip. Were they OSS agents traveling undercover? He finally had an opportunity to ask one of them about their mission. To his amazement, the group was on their way to test a new idea for the use of the 75mm cannon in a B-25 against tanks on the ground. Knowing the OSS as he did there was still doubt about their mission.

The trip to Casablanca was made without incident. It was easy to pass the time away sleeping since most of the trip was made by night. Upon arriving at Casablanca they were escorted to a small building on the edge of the airport. After a couple of days of literally doing nothing, they heard startling news. Colonel Mayhew was missing and was presumed to be dead. The plane he was aboard had crashed shortly after take off from Miami. The team had expected to meet Col. Mayhew in Casablanca, and he should have been here when they arrived. It was believed that his plane had gone down somewhere between 100 to 200 miles out of Miami. The last contact with the plane had been 100 miles out of Miami. The plane was not reported missing until it failed to reach Ascension Island. A couple of search planes from Ascension Island flew 300 miles of the route the plane should have been on for twelve hours, but no sign of life or wreckage of the plane was found. A further delay for the team could now be expected.

There was nothing for them to do but wait. During the long drawn out waiting period, they repeatedly discussed the possible causes of Col. Mayhew's death. The same questions went through each of their minds. What part would he have played in their mission? Would their mission be aborted? Where is Joseph?

Such questions were asked over and over without any of them being resolved, but they did get some information from a young pilot who flew transports from the states. The last radio transmission received from the missing plane, gave its location as 100 miles out of Miami. The plane was not reported missing until it was overdue at Ascension, and the authorities believed the plane had either missed the island, or had more than likely gone down prior to reaching the island. The transport pilot - who was on his way to Ascension 50 miles out of another airfield - saw what he thought at the time to be a shooting star, or maybe distant lightening. After hearing about the missing plane he told the team that he was now sure that was what he had seen. "If it was the plane," he asserted. "it was blown out of the sky." So the location of the crash would not be around Ascension Island, but off the coast of Florida one to two hundred miles. After hearing about the crash, the pilot reported what he saw to the authorities; they displayed little interest.

"If the explosion I saw was indeed the plane, there would have been no survivors."

"Do you think the Colonel's plane was sabotaged?" asked Rick.

"I wouldn't go that far, but I know it was not a normal crash. But you know, it's strange, there has been virtually no interest shown regarding an investigation as to the cause. Guess it will be chalked up as just another plane crash."

"Why would anyone want to get rid of Colonel Mayhew? Assuming it was sabotage."

"Could have been the Germans," replied Rick.

"If that were the case, then we had better be watching out, it could happen to us. Could there be a Trojan horse?"

"What do you mean Rick?"

"Forget it Tony."

As they discussed the many possibilities of why the plane crashed, they heard a jeep pull up outside. From the jeep they heard a familiar voice and were delighted to recognize it as Joseph's.

They rushed outside to greet the prodigal.

"Where have you been? They both asked at the same time. "I got real sick at my stomach and just couldn't fly when it was time to leave."

"Why didn't you tell us?"

"There wasn't enough time, it just hit me all at once."

"Did you hear about Colonel Mayhew?" asked Tony.

"No! What about Colonel Mayhew?"

"His plane exploded after taking off from Miami and all aboard went to the bottom of the ocean."

"How terrible." remarked Joseph. "What in the world could have happened?"

"The word around here is that it was a bomb, or at least some kind of an explosion on the plane."

Joseph looked down at the floor and in a slow and sympathetic voice remarked. "What a shame."

While it was not known in Casablanca, the war department had turned the matter over to Military Intelligence and the FBI. Plans were underway to make a thorough investigation of the plane crash. There was circumstantial evidence that the plane crash was anything but normal. Also the OSS demanded an investigation be made since Colonel Mayhew was on a Top Secret mission for them, then, such could have had a direct bearing on the crash.

After another day of delay, the Alamo team was

told they would leave Casablanca for Oran in six hours. No mention was made about a replacement for Colonel Mayhew. The team boarded a twin-engine plane loaded with miscellaneous supplies such as toilet paper, soap and the like.

"Makes me feel special to be on such an important flight," grinned Tony. The trip from Casablanca to Oran was about 400 miles. Captain Jim Kelly was the pilot. He had tried to get into combat aircraft but was assigned to the important job of moving low priority material along the supply lines in North Africa. He was from the state of Pennsylvania, which immediately bonded he and Rick as friends.

The plane shook and swayed in the turbulence of the heat rising above the desert floor as it cruised at 5,000 feet. As on former flights, there was nothing to do but sleep. The trip only required about three hours. After a short stopover at Oran, the plane was back in the air and on the way to Algiers.

Upon arriving at Algiers the C-47 was assigned to a holding pattern that continued for thirty minutes. While circling the landing field they observed twenty-four P-40 fighters taking off to the east. Finally the C-47 was given the clearance to land. The day was May 5, 1943. It was estimated that the war in Africa would be over by the time the team arrived in Algiers. The determined effort of the Germans at prolonging the war continued in Tunisia.

Captain Ellis met them at the airport with two jeeps. They were taken to a small building on the edge of the airport. The building held some semblance of a machine shop, with sleeping quarters attached. After unloading their gear, Captain Ellis took them to one of the mess halls, where they were served fresh coffee, scrambled egg substitute, and all the grits they could eat. It was the best meal they had had in days - the coffee was the best ever. After mess Captain Ellis told them that he had no orders for them other than for the team to hold tight and wait!

At 1100 hours the next morning Captain Ellis appeared with two British officers from MI-6. The British Major stood before the group in his shabby uniform that lacked the expected shine from the brass, and was in dire need of pressing. His hat must have been a reject from WWI.

"My name is Major Charles Anderson, and this is Captain Kenneth James. Captain James has been assigned to your team and will be with you until you relocate."

Captain James was well accepted by the Alamo team. He portrayed the look of a leader and gave the impression that he knew his business.

"I am glad to be with you yanks. I will assist you in every way I can." A soft-spoken Captain James stated. He continued, "I am aware of your loss and the loss to the American war effort in the death of Colonel Mayhew. I will try my best to fill in the void that he left. As you know the war continues in Tunisia, but the end is in sight - possibly just a few days."

This news brought cheers from the team. They had heard some criticism from the British about the Americans inability to fight and win.

"The Americans won't let the Germans keep them out of that town for long. As soon as the area is cleared of hostile troops we will continue to Bizerte where you will be issued your final equipment and clothing. I know you would like to write and let the folks back home know you are alright, but as far as the folks back home know you are still in the states, and that is the way it will have to remain - sorry."

Major Anderson stood and asked; "Are there any questions gentlemen?"

"Well," said Major Anderson, "since there are no questions you are dismissed. By the way may I wish you good hunting!"

After the brass left the meeting, Joseph looked at Tony with a disgusted look.

"Here we are in another town, briefed by two more brass hats, and we still know nothing - nothing!"

SIXTEEN

Captain James' driver brought over the captain's bedroll and bags. He would be with the team for a short time, but they had no idea what part he would play in their mission. When the team settled down that night Captain James gave them a great deal of information on the war in Africa, and some insight into the nightlife in Cairo, Egypt. He had been an aid to a Corps Commander while he was stationed in Cairo. He had the good fortune of staying at the famous Shepheard Hotel; Cairo's best.

"The most famous "belly dancer" in the world performed there," grinned Captain James.

"The food and the wine was of the finest, and the local girls were very friendly."

"Maybe we can get a pass and visit Cairo after our assignment," grinned Rick.

"Let's make it a date. I will show you around and make sure you see all the sights."

"We'll count on it Captain James." Agreed Tony.

On the morning of May 8th the news began to filter in that the Americans had taken Bizerte. The Germans were soundly whipped. The British were already in the city of Tunis, and by afternoon of the 9th it was confirmed. The cities of Bizerte and Tunis were completely in Allied hands. The war was over in North Africa - for all practical purposes. (The war did not end officially until May 13, 1943.)

Captain James was called away on the morning of May 10th and was gone until nearly noon. When he returned he had the news the team had been waiting for. They would move to Bizerte that afternoon.

The Alamo team was ready to move out by 1330. However it was decided that the team would fly to Tabarka, sixty miles west of Bizerte, and then move to Bizerte by land. Since the war was not officially over it was felt that the air space around Bizerte might not be safe for any type of plane since gun crews were still jumpy. The team would be flying over to Tabarka in a twin engine Lockheed - given to the British early in the war for use as a bomber. As the team loaded into the plane Captain James had a few words with the British pilot.

"There is one thing I have learned," said Joseph, "The British are a people of few words. I guess they know what they're doing, but it's a sure cinch we don't!"

With very little equipment, the team was aboard and ready for takeoff by 1600 hours. The flight to Tabarka required a little more than two hours. As soon as the plane came to a halt on the small runway there were two jeeps alongside and the team was instructed to load up. This would be their first extended ride in a jeep - a sixty miler. They were each given a scarf to tie around their mouth and nose to keep the sand from

going into their lungs. Goggles protected their eyes
from the constant shower of dust. Before they departed Captain James gave them M-1 carbines and two
fifteen round clips each for defense.

"We will be challenged several times on the road
before we reach Bizerte. Just let me handle it. If we
are fired upon along the road you will be told when to
fire back. Our main concern will be bands of Arabs
out on the road high jacking vehicles."

Other than being stopped at American and British
sentry posts along the way, the trip was uneventful.
At long last, the teamed arrived in Bizerte after midnight on the morning of May 11th. Here again they
were taken to an isolated location and left to themselves. Captain James was the first one to lie down on
a ground pallet, settling in for what remained of the
night.

At the crack of daylight, Captain James was up
for the day. He informed the team that he was going
out to find a field kitchen where they could get some
chow, especially hot coffee.

Although Bizerte was declared to be in American
hands, there was sporadic rifle and machine gun fire
in different spots around the area. In addition there
were several anti-aircraft guns fired during the night.
The town had sustained substantial bombing and
shelling by the Germans. Under the present conditions it was best to stay out of sight. After an hour
Captain James, and a helpful GI, returned in a jeep
with hot coffee, cold grits and more of those make
believe eggs.

"Hope you yanks appreciate my braving gunfire and mortar rounds to bring you this delicious breakfast."
"If it were possible we would recommend you for the Victoria Cross," laughed Rick.

After chow there were serious questions that all those present wanted answered, but Captain James was unable to give them satisfactory answers.
"What do we do now?"
"All we can do is to wait and stay off the streets. We are not going to be here for a long. We should know something by tomorrow.

On the afternoon of May 12th the team was alerted for movement. They were taken to a large building on the west side of the city where they were shown the Italian's equipment, and all the clothing and food supplies they could imagine. The capture of Italian troops had provided an enormous quantity of supplies and equipment. Civilian clothing had already been laid out for each member of the team. Everything from caps to underwear had to be authentic, as well as Italian cigarettes, matches, toothbrush, toothpaste, razors, etc.

"Remember how Italian cigarettes tasted Tony?" asked Joseph.
"Naw, but I smell the one you're smoking and I'm glad I don't remember," grinned Tony.

MI-6 would provide the explosives, radio, generator, and heavy weapons in the event they were needed. The team members were offered either a German lugar, or an Italian berretta for their own personal weapon. For the first time since leaving Virginia they had personal weapons. They selected the Italian berretta for their side arm. It was small and easy to carry and they were told it was more dependable than the luger.

The team met with Captain James late on the afternoon of May 13th for a final briefing. They would board a British submarine for their trip to Italy. Expected T.O.D. was 2100 hours. Tony could not believe it. Travel across the sea in a boat that goes under the water?
"Never in a million years!" he exclaimed to the group.
"You will never know it Tony, you'll be surprised at how smooth the ride will be."
"Rick! I am not going under water on any submarine, I can't take that."
"Tony, we'll get you some pills that'll make you sleep all the way to Italy. How will that do?"
"If I go on that submarine you will have to put me to sleep, I am not going unless you do."
Tony was not joking and Rick knew it!
Captain James heard the conversation and immediately knew that Tony was a victim of claustrophobia. The Captain decided to have a going away party before they boarded the sub making sure Tony took part in the celebration. 'Will we really have to drug poor Tony to get him aboard'? he wondered.

Arriving at the small battered dock, well after dark, the Alamo team remained out of sight while waiting for the submarine to make its appearance. Finally Captain James made contact with a British officer on the sub. After they had exchanged a few words, the team and equipment was loaded onto the submarine. The British sub captain explained to Tony that they would not go under the surface unless it was absolutely necessary for survival, and that problem would not have to be faced before the next day at the very earliest.

"You chaps can stand on the tower for the rest of the night if it will make you more comfortable."

Tony offered no more resistance.

The British submarine was the HMS Swordfish, K-class, capable of 15.5 knots on the surface and 10 knots below. It was 265 feet long and could dive to a depth of around 200 feet. It was armed with one 4" main gun, in addition to machine guns and torpedoes. However on this trip the torpedoes would be left behind to allow more room for the passengers and their equipment. The distance from Bizerte to their destination in Italy was about 280 plus nautical miles. Estimated T.O.A. (time of arrival) was 0300 hours May 15th.

It was 2110 hours when the sub moved away from the dock. The harbor was difficult to navigate because of the sunken ships and other debris scattered on the surface. Mines were a real danger as the harbor and the outer area had not been cleared completely. After careful navigation on the part of the submarine crew, the HMS Swordfish cleared the harbor and headed out to sea.

After the excitement of leaving Bizerte had subsided, Captain James called the Alamo team together for an in-depth briefing.

"I am going to give you a complete run down of your mission to the current extent of my knowledge. I will be glad to answer any questions you have provided I know the answers. I will accompany you to your destination, which will be the small town of Nettuno, in Italy, thirty-five miles below Rome. I am to make sure that you are picked up by your legitimate contact; not a German or Italian agent. This man is one of the top partisans in Italy. His name is Mario Berti, code name Titus. One of the top agents in this area is working with Titus and a couple of other groups. He is from MI-6; code name Suez. I will take you to the landing site to meet Titus, then I will return to the submarine."

"You will not go with us?"

"No, Tony, my orders are to return to Bizerte on the sub."

"Well, who in this man's army is going to tell us what we are to do in Italy?"

"Rick, we have sealed orders that are to be opened only when we have made contact with Titus, and of course the Italian shore."

"Oh, I see; that's when we'll know." Rick answered thoughtfully.

The night was dark and the water calm. The Alamo team enjoyed the beauty of a night on the Mediterranean Sea while standing on the cunning tower.

"How do you like the view Tony?"

"This is my kind of a trip, Joseph."

Daylight came early on the morning of May 14.

For several hours the sub continued on the surface with lookouts at all stations. After a scare, caused by an unidentified aircraft, the submarine submerged for the remainder of the day. Tony had adjusted to living below the surface and found it no different than being up on the surface, as long as he didn't think about it.

There were the usual card games, and plenty of good coffee, supplied by the U.S. Army. The British love their tea, but as far as the Americans were concerned they could have it!

As the night of the 14th closed in, the submarine crew, and its passengers, became more closed mouth and nervous. The water near the Italian mainland could be well patrolled by German and/or Italian boats. There was also the ever present danger of running into uncharted mine fields. The major concern of the mission would be the possibility of being discovered by the enemy at the time of landing.

At 2300 hours the sub received a transmission from Oran. Strict orders had been issued for radio silence before they departed, and now those who issued the orders were disobeying them.

Captain James was summoned to the sub captain's quarters. The messages were decoded and read, then handed to Captain James. He could not believe the message - yet it seemed very authentic. The message read as follows:
Captain James you are to accompany the Alamo team on their mission. Your code name will be Robin. Captain James looked at the sub commander in dis-

belief.

"What is it, chap?

"Robin is my wife's name"

After a long pause Captain James spoke in a low voice as though thinking out loud.

"They gave me that name to assure me the message was official. Does Robin know that I am out here?" he mumbled to himself.

The Alamo team had been in the "sack" for an hour when Captain James awakened them with the news of his new assignment.

"I don't know what this means, nor why my orders were changed, but at least I am with a good team."

"Does this mean you are in charge of the team now, Captain?"

Rick was to lead the American team and work with any others the team might be attached to. At least, that was the way it was when they left Washington.

"I don't know for sure Rick, but at any rate I'm sure we can work together, right?"

"No problem from our team, Captain."

No one said anything for a few minutes. Finally Captain James broke up the meeting with these encouraging words.

"We'll be landing in a few hours, let's try to get some sleep."

At 0130, the team was alerted to rise with a rather brisk shaking.

"It's time. Landing will be at 0300."

"What is our position?" one asked sleepily.

"Fifteen miles off shore."

The team assembled their equipment at the bottom of the hatch and headed for the kitchen. They were served eggs, hash browns, toast, and coffee for their final meal aboard the sub.

While they had been eating, the sub had slowly moved toward land and was now within three miles of the landing sight.

At 0215 the sub surfaced and slowly headed closer to the shore. The night was black with only a few dim lights visible from the shore. Not a sound could be heard. Every ear was strained for the drumming motor of an enemy patrol boat lurking in the area. The diesel engines started turning slowly and pushed the sub within 800 yards of the shore. The lookouts declared the area safe after another long period of silence and strained ears. Lights were dimmed below deck as the team climbed the ladders to topside. Rubber boats had been inflated, and their equipment was being loaded. The English sailors would paddle the boats to the beach. In a low voice the sub captain patted each man on the back with the same comment to each.

"Good luck, and good hunting!"

Captain James lingered for just a few moments and had a few words with the sub captain. The conversation was in such low tones, it could only be heard by the two of them. Maybe it was a word for his wife to be passed along. After all this man would simply drop out of sight and sound from the world, and who knew when he would ever return. Maybe he at least wanted his wife to have an idea of his demise, if indeed this did come to pass.

THE PLAN was as follows: The sub was to wait for one and one half hours for the rubber boats to return. If they had not returned in that time the sub would pull out to sea. If the sub was discovered it was to immediately pull away and head for deep water. Those out of the sub would have to fend for themselves.

While the paddles pulled the little rubber boats through the calm waters toward the beach, they remained in utter silence. Only the paddles were making more noise than the heartbeats of those aboard the little vessels.

Each man was left to his own thoughts - a time for reflection. Tony had mixed emotions. It had been years since he had seen the town of Nettuno and the surrounding countryside - his home country. He thought about Betty and wondered if he would ever see her again. She wouldn't care; she had no doubt forgotten all about him. Maybe he should go over the hill and just stay in Italy.

Captain James could only think about his wife and how she would react to his disappearance. Would she think he was dead? Maybe take the first offer of marriage? Would she wait for years for the war to end even though she knew nothing of his last mission?

Joseph wondered audibly, "If I get caught by the Germans will they shoot me because I'm a Jew or because I'm a spy." He understood his position should he be caught. He had a way out, as did the others if they chose not to be tortured - the cyanide capsule. He was the only one that voiced his thoughts so that all could hear.

'Strange,' thought Rick, 'was he trying to get sympathy, or maybe make a case?'

The boats were almost to the shore. Every eye was straining to see through the darkness. The all-consuming question on each one's mind was, would they face friend are foe? This was the most dangerous and nerve-racking time of the entire mission so far. Who was beyond the darkness? The little boats were pulled onto the sand covered beach and nestled between two twenty-foot fishing boats. Luckily the fishing boats were unoccupied, and the beach appeared completely abandoned. The time was now 0315.

The signal into the darkness was two, two second flashes from one flashlight. The signals were sent and now the wait. They peered into the darkness, holding their guns in readiness. They did have the protection of the two fishing boats, which helped them to stay out of sight. Minutes went by; no return signal. The team was on edge. The danger at this stage of the game would be for someone to react to a noise or movement and give their position away.

Captain James put a coat over his wristwatch and flashed a light on it to see the time. It was now 0330 hours. Fifteen minutes had passed and still nothing. Had someone gone for the Italian or German troops? They still had remaining time before having to make a major decision, but time was running out. Any minute they could be discovered by German or Italian soldiers, or by some of the civilians living near by. The suspense was unbearable.

The silence was broken by the sound of one or more persons walking toward them on the sand. Was this the partisan contact? The man walked as though he might be under the influence, although the sand could have caused him to walk unsteadily.

"Tony, when the man gets here and discovers us, ask him what he is doing, and if he is from Titus?"

"Rick, load the crossbow just in case we can't deal with this man."

The man seemed surprised when he stumbled onto the group huddled around his fishing boat.

"What are you doing here?" Asked Tony.

"I came down here to get my boat to go fishing. Who are you people, Germans?" At that moment he flashed his light, and by chance it hit Captain James directly in the face. He yelled, "Americans, Americans." As he proclaimed his discovery he began to run away from the group toward the town. They knew if he got to town with the news that Americans were on the beach, their lives would not be worth a nickel.

"Rick!" barked Captain James, "get him!" The cross bow was quiet and efficient.

"How could he have known we were Americans?" They all asked in unison.

"That has been a puzzle to me," pondered Captain James.

"I'm afraid he saw my cap and thought it was part of an American uniform."

Captain James had not had time to change into his civilian clothing. His spare clothes were packed, so he thought it best to wait until they reached the shore in the event he got wet. However, he had been secretly holding onto the hope that his orders were a mistake and would be changed at the last minute.

Another check of the time added anxiety to the already tense situation. It was 0340. It was now only moments until decision time for everyone.

After the scare it was decided to station someone about twenty-five yards or so in the direction of town. If anyone came toward the group maybe they could be turned back. Tony was given the assignment.

Tony stationed himself in a small dug out place in the sand and waited. He did not have long to wait. He heard approaching footsteps like those of a woman since they were light and short. When the figure was close enough, Tony reached out and pulled it down. To his surprise, this was not a woman, but a young boy. Tony took the boy back to the group. Tony asked him to explain his presence on the beach, but he said nothing. Before the second question could be asked the boy made a gesture with his hands and started walking away.

"What should we do with him," asked Tony.

"Let him go Tony. We have nothing to lose since time is running out. It's a risk, but that's what we get paid for."

With the disappearance of the young boy into the darkness there was dead silence. After an ample lapse of time they checked their watches. It was now

0355, and the boy had not returned. It was decided to move the rubber boats into the surf and be ready to make a quick exit. Although a silent thought, it was unanimous; they had been set up. It was now 0400 as the little boats were pushed into the water for the trip back to the sub. As they started paddling, they saw two two-second flashes of light from the shore.

Captain James ordered his boat back to shore, but the other to remain off shore just in case. When the little rubber boat came close to the beach there were four men and a boy standing in the surf.

"I am Titus," spoke a voice from the group.

"We have been waiting for you since midnight. We were informed that you would be here at 0100. When you did not show up we were afraid that you might have been intercepted and the Germans had set a trap for us. You know we have lost several good men in the last month due to betrayal from within. We sent the boy down to see if you were the real team or one the Germans had planted."

No other words were exchanged as the equipment was quickly removed from the boats, and the British crews were promptly dispatched to the waiting sub.

"We must hurry," said Titus. "It will be daylight in a very short time and we must clear the beach and town before we can be spotted. There are few German troops in the area, but the Gestapo has spies on every corner. The Germans do not trust the Italians and the Italians do not trust the Germans."

"Captain!" Titus said, speaking in a low but stern

tone; "You must change your clothes before we move inland. You will be much better off being shot as a spy than a British officer with a bunch of spies."

"Right chap, I will."

Titus could speak understandable English on most occasions. When necessary Tony could fill in the missing words. The other three members of the group could only speak and understand Italian, with a little German for good measure. One of the men knew the De Angelo family when they lived near Cisterna.

The group now consisted of eight. The boy was sent away since his part of the mission was complete. Such a group would certainly attract someone's attention, and turn the group in. The local people were suspicious of any outsiders. The Germans had infiltrated various partisan groups that resulted in many being killed or taken prisoner.

After moving a distance from the beach into an isolated location, Titus showed the group a crude handmade map showing the route they would be taking. They would move along the small narrow road until daylight. This should put them in the vicinity of the little village of LeFerriere. If they made excellent time, they could possibly reach the west branch of the Mussolini Canal. There they could spend the day in hiding. After dark they would proceed along the canal until it reached the main branch of the Mussolini Canal, which ran southeast. The main branch of the canal was very wide and its bank offered a good surface to walk on. The canal would take them close to Cori. Once in the hills they would be securely hidden. Their hideout would be a small farm consisting of one house with a small barn. Only one road ran from Cori out past the farm, and if the Germans or Italians tried to surprise them, it would be very easy to escape into the hills, or even block the road for a short period of time. So much for the plans, they thought, now to execute them and not get caught.

The trip was long and exhausting, but after reaching the Mussolini Canal the team settled down for the first day inside the banks of the west branch. They were all bone tired. As each made a spot to sleep and rest, Tony began to tell about the places his father had worked, and the many trips he had made as a water boy. Even though the mosquitoes were having a field day performing transfusions on the group, they were too tired to resist. Tony found himself alone with his thoughts as the others dropped off one by one. The years he had spent in this part of Italy with his family and friends seemed a lifetime ago. Cisterna was only six miles up the road making it tempting for Tony to slip off for a visit when he could get away. As he dropped off to sleep memories of his childhood drifted in and out.

Cori was twenty miles from Nettuno. With only about 15 miles left, they planned to make it to their base the following night. At dusk they loaded their gear onto their backs, making sure to bury all cans and debris before they moved out.

As the group came to the intersection of Highway 7 and the Mussolini Canal, they spotted an Italian

Army checkpoint.

"This has been added in just the past few days," Titus explained.

"Do you think they are looking for us?"

"No Captain, they set these road blocks up at different times and different places. They are looking for deserters and black marketeers primarily."

"What do you think we should do, Titus?"

"We will have to wait for complete darkness, then try to cross 200 yards to the south."

"Why not go under the bridge? Some asked.

"They have probably laid anti-personal mines across the canal to make sure no one could cross under the bridge, without being blown up. After a few seconds of thought, Captain James verbalized the sentiment of the entire group, "We will wait."

Once in total darkness, one of Titus' men went to check the road 200 yards to the south. He returned quickly with good news. No Italian troops, or anyone else, along the road.

"We must hurry," explained Titus. "Cross the road one at time, waiting one hundred yards on the other side until we all make it across."

Three of the men had made it across safely when they heard vehicles coming up the road toward them. Everyone flattened down trying to hide from view. To the amazement of the group, three vehicles stopped along the road directly between the two groups. Tony and Captain James were waiting at the edge of the road to cross, and could hear every word spoken by the Italian soldiers.

"What are they stopping for, Tony? Are they looking for us?"

"Naw," said Tony in a muffled voice. "They have some women in the trucks and don't want the commanding officer at the bridge to know it."

In a hushed voice, "We have got to move Captain, or they will see us."

They went back to the group and explained the situation.

They had three options.

Titus offered a couple.

"We can kill them, which is the last resort, or we can hope they walk away and not see us."

Tony added the third option.

"If they see us we can go along with them and try to buy sex, and time, until the rest of the group gets across the road safely, then punch them out, take their money, and they will just think they have been rolled."

So three of Titus's men went to the women and did an excellent job. The women would have a sore jaw, but they were lucky, they could be dead.

The women were camp followers, probably from the Naples area. Their pimp would not believe it when they told him they had no money.

The plan worked, and by daylight the team had made it to the hills, and the farm, outside Cori.

Mario Berti (Titus) was well known around Cori. He had connections that would give the team access to many valuable contacts. The team would live in the barn, and be supplied with food and information by

Titus and his group. Now that they had reached their destination, it was time to find out what exactly their assignment was. Captain James had been given a sealed envelope when the team departed the submarine. It was not to be opened until they had reached their destination.

While the team was getting settled the radio was set up for the important message to be relayed to Washington. The following message was sent to London, then to Canada, and on to the OSS in Virginia.

"Alamo is well. There are seven reasons why."

SEVENTEEN

Betty had been in Canada for a couple of weeks on her old radio watch job. When the message came in that "Alamo is well", Betty was not on watch. Everyone knew she was vitally interested in the Alamo team, and continued to believe that Tony was a member. Shown the message, the obvious question was, what does "seven reasons" mean? No one could answer her question. She was to find out later in Washington that "seven reasons" was a code name for the seven hills around Rome. If, indeed, Tony is a member of Alamo, then he is in Rome. What could he be doing in Rome? She wondered.

Betty was on her second tour of duty in Canada. When she was previously there she met a handsome captain from the Canadian Army who took a special interest in her. They had a few dates and met a few times for coffee while on the job. She had never been serious about him; in fact she could not remember his last name when they met for the second time. This was not a problem for this dashing Captain. He came onto her like a hurricane - much more aggressive than at their first meeting. His name was

Richard Hamilton, but he liked to be called Rick. Betty tried to keep their association on a somewhat impersonal basis so she always called him Richard. Although Betty was still in love with Tony, (she was, wasn't she?), it was getting harder and harder to turn Richard down for dates when apparently all he wanted was her company.

There wasn't much to do for entertainment in that part of Canada. There was a small bar or two, equipped with a jukebox. The popular reason to go there was to hear American music. It helped to listen to music from home. The most popular records were those of Glenn Miller and Harry James. Betty loved to dance, but she had a problem with Richard because he wanted to do more serious dancing - holding too close - rather than dance to the faster tempos Betty preferred.

At times Richard would say something that was not called for, and reading between the lines, Betty knew that sooner or later the show down would come and she would have to make a decision. Richard would hang around her workstation when he was off duty and would even try and kiss her when he thought he could. One of her supervisors saw him kiss her lightly one night and gave Betty the riot act. "You know Miss Peterson, such conduct is not tolerated while on duty!"
"Yes, Major."
"You know such activity is "off limits." Betty knew the woman was just jealous.
It was much easier for her to say Richard was off lim-

its than for Betty to make him "off limits."

Richard Hamilton was 6'2", weighed 185, with a small black mustache, dark brown eyes, and a smile that complemented all of his other physical attributes.

One of the big parties of the year was coming up the next week. It was the Base Commander's Summer Fling. Richard had been talking about it for some time. He made Betty commit to going several times over the past few days. Betty had never attended this party, so she was looking forward to it. Richard had promoted it as though it was the only party of the year. Although many of the women who would attend were in the military, on this special occasion they would be permitted to wear their favorite evening gowns. A fifteen piece Canadian band would provide the music, and would play mostly American music.

As Richard was leaving the office he turned back at the door, again reminding Betty,

"Don't forget, I'll pick you up promptly at seven."

"I won't forget Richard, I will be ready."

Betty had been attending such special parties from the time she had attended Central High School and Vanderbilt. She had always been on the defensive to some extent, because it seemed with all special events there was for some reason a feeling by the male gender that something special should happen. 'Was this the night Richard would make his big move?' She wondered. If he did, could she resist him? Or even more frightening, would she? It really came down to one important issue. Did she still really love Tony?

By all appearances everyone turned out for the "Summer Fling". There were a few Americans sprinkled among the many Canadians at the party. The music was just like one would hear down in the states. The food was a little different from the Washington, D.C. fare, but very tasty.

Richard had danced most every dance with Betty. There were a few times he could not ignore a break from some of the high-ranking officers in attendance. They shared a table with another couple, who were as much in love as a couple could possibly be. As the party wound down the couple left and Richard and Betty were alone for the first time. Now Richard could get Betty's undivided attention.

Richard took Betty's hands into his, looked deep into her blue eyes for what seemed an eternity, then asked,

"Betty, will you marry me?"

Betty's heart started beating so hard that she knew Richard could hear it, or could feel the table shaking. Her face was flushed - her hands cold. She was not prepared for this.

He continued, "You know that we get along great together; we are meant for each other. I have loved you since the first time I laid eyes you."

He waited for some form of response, but Betty could only sit in shock, utterly speechless.

"If you had rather wait for a while to give me your answer, that's alright with me. I am willing to wait," he said with a painful expression. His soft brown eyes looked like a little boy who wanted something special for Christmas.

For the first time since they had started going together Betty saw Richard in a different light. Perhaps she was in love with him but hadn't realized it. What was she to do? Tony had never left her mind or her heart. If there had been no Tony, she would have said yes to Richard, but when she compared her feelings for the two, she knew in her heart she just could not marry anyone but Tony.

"Richard, dear Richard, your proposal is more than flattering, and I really am fond of you, maybe more that I realized."

Without waiting for another word from Betty.

"For that reason you should say yes. You are the most beautiful - yes, the most gorgeous woman I have ever laid my eyes on. We could be totally happy together."

"Richard you know there is someone else in my life, and no matter how hard I try, I cannot forget him nor stop loving him; I am sorry."

"Don't give me a final answer tonight Betty, think it over for a few days."

"You are sweet, kind, and considerate Richard, and I will always hold you in my heart as a dear friend, but the answer will always be no, I am truly sorry."

For Betty and Richard the party was over. There was nothing left to say. Richard left Betty at her door with a short, but warm, kiss and a "good night."

While it was only a little past midnight, the night had seemed like an eternity to Betty. She tried to go to sleep, but sleep was impossible. Did she make a mistake by turning Richard down? Did she really love Tony that much? She hadn't seen him in months. Maybe it was just infatuation rather than love. Over and over she had tried to think it through. As she looked at the clock at 4:00 a.m. one thing became very clear, she had to get out of Canada and back to Washington for a new assignment.

As the days went by she invariably ran into Richard at least once or maybe twice a day, and each time he was wearing that same hurt look on that handsome face, making her feel like a crumb. Maybe she should have put him off and not crushed him like a tender flower. If she could get out and away it would be easier on him and she would not continually feel so guilty.

After eight days of waiting, Betty got her orders to report back to DC for a new assignment. The news spread rapidly around the base that Betty and a couple other Americans were leaving. Richard did not want it to be true, but after checking with the base commander's office, it was confirmed. Betty dreaded having to face him for the last time. She could not be expected to defend against those soft brown eyes forever.

"Just dropped by to say goodbye, Betty.""Richard I don't know what to say, other than I wish you the best of everything and a safe war."

"Yeah, a safe war."

Richard made a move to embrace Betty, but she backed off.

"Richard, it would be best for both of us if we just

shook hands, and parted as friends."
With a deep look into each other's eyes - as though searching for something satisfying - they parted without saying a word.

Betty boarded the plane with a couple of American officers and two other women. One was from England, the other from Canada. They introduced themselves and settled down for the flight.

After fifteen minutes of staring at Betty, one of the women shouted above the roar of the engines.
"Say, aren't you the one that was dating Captain Hamilton?"
"Yes," shouted Betty, "We had several dates."
"You dated that "hunk" and you are going back to the states without him!"
"Yes, I am going back to the states without him."
"How could you do it? He is the number one hunk in the world."
Betty thought to herself. 'Yes, how could she do it; the number one hunk in the world.'

EIGHTEEN

It was now time for the Alamo team to find out about their objective. After all, they had traveled a long way and endured much adversity to reach their final destination. No one had a clue as to the exact mission. They had guessed some form of sabotage, or maybe they were to train some of the Italian partisans. When the real mission was finally revealed, they were astounded.

Captain James was given a coded message as the team debarked from the submarine, to be read when they reached their destination. The time had arrived for that fateful moment.

The seal was broken and the paper folded so that everyone could see it. There was a page full of numbers that made no sense.

2-12-6 26-9-22 7-12 26-8-8-18-13-26-7-22
13-22-9-12   17-6-15-2-30 1943 2-12-6-9 24-12-13-
7-26-24-7   4-18-15-15 25-22 8-6-22-1 14-18-6 25-
20-22-13-7

The message was in alphabet code, rather than cryp-

tograph. Normally, coding would be on the crypto-
graph machine, but because of their mission, such a
secret coding machine could be lost, therefore, they
could not use it. The alphabet code would be the
most confusing to decode if in the wrong hands. The
message was to be destroyed as soon as it was read.
The key to reading the code was to understand where
in the alphabet the code began. The letter A would be
26 and the letter Z would be 1.
Captain James handed the coded message to Rick for
decoding. The message read.

YOU ARE TO ASSINATE NERO BEFORE JULY 30,
1943. YOUR CONTACT WILL BE SUEZ MI-6 AGENT.

Tony was the first to ask. "Who is Nero?"
In addition to a white capsule, Rick was given a pink
capsule that was to be opened when they reached
their destination. He pushed the heel of is shoe to the
side and removed the pink capsule. Removing a small
piece of paper and unfolding it - he read this message.
Nero is Benito Mussolini.
The team was in shock!
"Wow" exclaimed Tony. "How can it be done?" They all
stood in silence.
"Where is this Suez? Maybe he has the answers."
Had the team known all the facts about Mussolini,
and his close calls with death, they would have cried
insanity at the idea of getting rid of the great dictator.
There had been at least three attempts on his life.

One such attempt came close when the bullet grazed the Il Duce's nose.

The next day found them in deep discussions centered on their target. Titus joined them, accompanied by an Englishman by the name of Major John Cooper (code name Suez), a member of British Intelligence MI-6. He was introduced to everyone and seemed to be a very likeable chap.

As he stood talking he radiated a great deal of confidence in his ability to get things done. This was a confidence builder for the team for they needed experienced leadership at this point in their mission. He had only been in Italy for a short time, but had spent some time around Rome listening to the people talk and mainly to determine if they were in a mood to revolt.

Rick got around to asking the question that was a puzzle to everyone.

"Why is it important to knock off the big guy?"

"That is a good question Rick, and I will try to tell you and the team what I have been told on this subject.

Benito Mussolini is the dictator of Italy. If such a person is eliminated, then the body is without a head. This can, and usually does, bring on unrest, followed by a civil war."

The Major continued with invaluable background material concerning Benito Mussolini.

"Mussolini was born in July 1883. His education was above average, but his family was poor. He became a very capable schoolteacher. As many aspiring leaders in Europe at that time in history he was looking for someone, or something, to hang on to - to emulate. For years he wrote for a newspaper and was opposed to Italy having any part of World War I. However during the war he changed his mind after studying the writings of Karl Marx. He joined the army and shortly after sustained a wound.

As early as 1918 he was advocating rule by dictatorship. He organized an assorted group of disenchanted people, forming a force he called Fasci di Combattimento. Thus was born the Fascist Party of Italy. True to his beliefs he insisted on force to rule rather than laws made by the people. He preached unrest and continually criticized the government. In the summer of 1922 a general strike was called. Mussolini demanded the government prevent the strike or the Fascists would. With 40,000 of his followers he made a threat in Naples to the effect that unless the government was willingly turned over to the Fascist Party, the party would march on Rome and take it forcibly. King Victor Emmanuel III gave in to Mussolini, whereby he became the youngest Prime Minister in Italian history. He came out of the same environment of strikes, unrest, and riots as did Adolf Hitler. The people welcomed the dictator state. The elections of 1924 secured the control of all government to the Fascist Party. The security of any dictator is to keep the people busy. If things are not going well at home, create interests in some other area. If promises made were not fulfilled, make more promises to be fulfilled at a future time. Mussolini did create jobs and projects that were good for the people.

From this vantage point we are in a position to clearly view any activity in and around the cities of Cisterna, Anzio, and Aprilia (the factory). You might be familiar with some of those projects. The people did prosper, enjoyed law and order, and welcomed the freedom from those wretched strikes. Mussolini was hailed as a genius by leaders in Europe, and in the United States, prior to the Allies entering the war."

Each member of the team hung on his every word with fascination as he continued,
"Dictators are ambitious people. Dictators are ambitious and extremely aggressive. They attain power through violence and threats and must maintain that atmosphere to exist. The people must continually be involved in local programs of benefit to their well-being, and activities of unrest to keep their minds on possible military campaigns. So in October 1935 Italy invaded Abyssinia, Africa. Then in 1935 and 1936 Italy continued its aggression by invading Ethiopia. The people of Italy were in full support of their leader. Italy now had established an empire. Not quite equal to the Roman Empire of long ago, but at least there was now a beginning. Mussolini promised the Italian people recognition, respect, and power - another Empire.

During the 30's another dictator had established himself - Hitler of Germany. It was only natural that they become partners. Hitler and Mussolini formed the Rome-Berlin Axis.

On June 10, 1940 Italy jumped into the fight that Hitler had begun by invading Poland. In September of 1939 he declared war on the opponents of Germany. Although Hitler and Mussolini appeared to be close friends, the truth was, they were just the opposite. Hitler had little respect for the ability of the Italians to do anything successful militarily. He did not confide in Mussolini, nor let him know of Germany's military plans. This lack of communication became a problem, and quite an embarrassment for IL Duce to have to play second fiddle to anyone, even Hitler.

Taking a back seat for so long - even to Hitler - was not the life style of IL Duce. So, in October of 1940 Mussolini sent his troops into Greece without informing Hitler of his intentions. The big invasion backfired when the Greeks pushed the Italians out of Greece into Albania. By mid December they occupied one third of Albania. This was an embarrassment for Hitler and his allies. The Fuhrer could not allow his reputation, nor his partner in crime, to suffer. With little notice the Germans moved into Albania, and on into Greece in the early part of 1941. History repeated itself in Africa, compelling Hitler to rush to the aid of Mussolini and his troops to prevent another disaster. As long as Hitler was able to hold the Allies at bay in North Africa, Mussolini seemed to be in control in Italy. However, the campaign in North Africa ended in defeat for both the Germans and Italians. This defeat resulted in hundreds of thousands of Italians being detained in prisoner of war camps for the remainder of the war. This was May, 1943 and by now the Italians at home were disenchanted with the war, in particular, Mussolini."

Slowly pacing the floor, Suez continued, "I have not been told the exact location, but there's going to be another invasion somewhere in the Mediterranean area. This will further weaken the government of Mussolini. Our mission must be completed before this operation can be attempted. The people of Italy are ready to overthrow this dictator and his government, but lack the power. Such a government can be overthrown if the head is removed, as I mentioned at the outset. So if Mussolini can be removed, then those in charge of the government will sue for peace. There are many German troops in Italy. The Gestapo has become more active in Italy making the work of the partisans much more dangerous. The operation that I refer to, if successful, should bring an end to German and Italian troop opposition - if an invasion should occur. The German troops will withdraw from Italy, and the Italian troops will lay down their arms.

You can see that we have a very important mission to carry out and if successful will shorten the war and save many lives of both American and British soldiers.

Any questions on the background information I have supplied?"

"When do we get started," asked Tony.

"I hope everyone is as enthused as Tony and ready to get started. Now let's hear from Titus and the situation as he sees it on the local level."

"Can we expect the majority of the Italian population to be for or against us Titus?"

"That's a complicated question Rick. We have some

very faithful people who can be trusted. But a few have traded sides and informed the Gestapo or the Fascist Secret Police of our operations, often causing a loss of several of our top agents. My advice is to trust only those who have previously proven themselves. Recently one of our best agents turned in three of our people in Rome. The Germans had taken his daughter from his home, while searching houses within one of their infamous roadblocks. Being Germans they knew how to use her. They issued an ultimatum to him: her life or his cooperation. He compromised, but in the end he was killed, along with his daughter and three other agents. War is a terrible experience for civilians as well as soldiers."

The final organization for the assassination of Mussolini was now complete; consisting of Impala, Falcon, Kite, Titus, Suez, and Robin. To complete their mission by July 30th would require every moment of the time they had remaining, and then some. There were many obstacles to work through; the greatest being to locate their target and intercept it at the proper time. Since Tony could speak the native dialect and knew the territory, it was decided to let him take Captain James and Rick to scout the area. Titus and Suez would head for Rome to make contacts with the partisans and try to come up with a plan for their mission. They would all meet back at the barn just outside of Cori in three weeks.

NINETEEN

Days felt like months since Betty had returned to Washington from her fruitless trip to the OSS camp in Virginia looking for Tony. While she had not given up, there was a desire to get an assignment out of the country.

During the summer of 1943, Washington, DC was the place to be if one relished the excitement generated by a huge military presence, and the continuous influx of unattached females flowing to Washington looking for a good government job.

Betty began dating Roger, a captain from Memphis that she preferred being with more than the other men who called for dates. They went to the Mayflower Hotel and made an effort to dance to the music of Harry James and his orchestra, but standing in one place and letting the crowd push you around was about the extent. They had a good time, but it was not as romantic as the young captain had hoped. Betty had intended to be more interested in her date and make the evening more pleasant, until she recognized a man she had previously talked to in an effort to locate Tony. A rush of adrenalin filled her whole being as she agonized, 'I must ask him about operation Alamo. I must get to him, but how?'

Betty abruptly asked Roger to dance with her. Her every intention was centered on reaching the table occupied by this man whom she felt was her only hope. By leading Roger, rather than being led, they made their way across the dance floor to his table. This was an unbelievable opportunity. However, once she had completed the maneuver, what could she say? Think! Think!

With sugary charm she cooed, "It's so good to see you again. How have you been?" Looking straight down into his eyes. Stunned by her greeting, he could only stare, at once recognizing her beauty. Everyone at the table looked at Betty in astonishment.

"Roger would you mind if I danced with an old friend for just one dance?" She purred.

"Of course not Betty," Roger replied in dismay.

Betty took the hand of the gentlemen at the table and started pulling him up out of his chair. She turned to the lady sitting to his left, "Do you mind?"

"Of course not as long as you leave this good looking young man in exchanged. You can dance with him all night," she laughed.

The man stood up hesitantly with his eyes riveted on Betty.

"I will dance with you, but I don't believe I know you."

"Oh sure you do. Don't you remember, we met at the company party some weeks back"

"If you say so."

"Don't you remember, you were telling me about an

operation called Alamo."

"Me? Not me. I never heard of such an operation in my entire life."

Betty's heart stopped. She could not believe what she was hearing. Flashbacks kept pulsing in her head, 'the difference between tonight and the last time we met - yeah, that's it - that night he was drinking and tonight he's almost sober.'

"Oh, you know," pleaded Betty, "they had a camp in Virginia somewhere."

"Lady, I believe you have the wrong guy. I know nothing about a camp in Virginia. Perhaps we had better return to my table and sit this one out."

Betty felt her face flush with embarrassment. Roger looked at her as though he could kill her with his bare hands. He was mad and ready to take her home. She had made a fool of him by her making a play for an older man that she obviously hardly knew. The night was a complete wash out.

Days had turned into weeks without a response to her request for an out of the country assignment. Betty had given up, when out of the blue she received a phone call instructing her to appear at the chief's office at 0900 the next morning.

At 0900 precisely she was ushered into the office, but to her surprise two strange men were seated near the chief's desk. They nodded at her as she sat down. They tried desperately to remain cool in the presence of her breathtaking beauty, but it was hard for the two men to avoid looking at Betty, she was some dish. They just wanted to enjoy the moment.

Finally the chief arrived with two of his agents. Introductions were made, but Betty only heard that one man was Mac and the other David.

"You will get to know them better in the future Betty." Explained the chief.

Jack Krum, the chief, propped himself against the front of his desk. After looking at each one of them for a full minute, he began.

"I appreciate the dedication of the members of the OSS who have completed tough jobs in the past. Now we have another difficult job to complete. As you are aware the United States has many areas that are considered high risk. Possibly the most important, and perhaps the most exposed of these, is the Panama Canal. If the canal could be destroyed, or even put out of service for a long period of time, it would critically cripple our ability to fight a war in the Pacific or the Atlantic. Troops have been stationed in the Canal Zone for years. During the past few years the zone has been beefed up so that the canal can be protected from any ground forces that might attack it. Japan is a long way off and it is not felt that the canal is in danger of an attack such as hit Pearl Harbor. It is not impossible to think that one lone small carrier could sneak in to striking distance of the canal, but this would be highly unlikely. Sabotage is now our number one concern, or, perhaps a coordinated effort from one of the small countries in the area. German agents have been very active in a couple of these countries. The FBI has tried to penetrate some of the organizations operating in one of these countries without success. To be honest we have lost four agents in the past five months. We know the leader of the most active and dangerous organization. When we do get one of our agents inside we find out very little. It's as though they know the agents' identity even before he is accepted as a member. It has become necessary to work out some other method of penetrating this organization.

We have strong evidence that an airstrip is being built in flying range of the canal. It is highly possible for the Germans or the Japanese to ship some medium range bombers into this country that could easily be flown to the canal. You probably already know that one country south of the canal is bordered by both the Pacific and Atlantic Oceans. This makes it reachable for either German or Japanese planes. It is highly unlikely that the west coast, which faces the Pacific Ocean, could be used for an airstrip, since the mountains are very rugged and high. Therefore it is almost certain that if such an airstrip is being constructed it would have to be on the east side of Columbia, fronted by the Caribbean Sea. There is a large area from Panama's southern border east along the coast of Columbia, with several possible landing places. There could conceivably be approximately 200 miles open and accessible for use by an enemy. The last agent down there had confirmed this possibility. He succeeded in getting a job with a company working in the jungle, and felt pretty confident that they might be building an airstrip. Although he left town for the construction site with other workers, he was never heard from again. We must assume he met with foul play.

Perhaps you have guessed by now that you three are going to get involved in some way with the defense of the canal. If that is what you are thinking you are one hundred percent correct. We have a plan that will require bravery and dedication for it to be carried out.

As you might already know the Federal Bureau of Investigation (FBI) has the same responsibility of protecting the canal from subversives as it does in the United States. Since the Bureau has been unsuccessful with male agents, it is felt that there is a good chance that a female agent could possibly gain entrance to the inside of the ring that is giving us the most concern. It's an obvious situation for a good-looking female agent, but the FBI had none. For that reason the FBI and the OSS will cooperate in this operation. As you may have no doubt noticed, we have the best looking female agent in the OSS right here in this room. She is smart, experienced, and very capable of successfully carrying out this difficult task. Gentlemen, let me introduce you to Betty Peterson.

"Hi Betty, I'm Mac. I can only agree with what has been said about you."

"Betty, I am David. You have to watch Mac, he has a weakness for blondes."

"I am glad to meet both of you and I hope you will always be as kind to me as you have been today."

"Now that we have the pleasantries taken care of let's go to the flip side."

Betty looked at the chief with a sudden feeling of apprehension.

"Now Betty, this will be a voluntary assignment on your part. You do not have to accept it. I want you to know this before I go any farther. As I go over the plans in detail you can be thinking about your part in this plan and assess the plus and minus sides. We need your input, so don't be bashful."

Mac raised his hand.

"I have a question in regard to the submarine threat to the canal. Can the Germans really move into that area with submarines?"

"I am afraid they can. In 1942 German submarines sank 270 ships in the Canal Zone."

"Can German submarines transport earth moving equipment into the area?" Asked David.

"No, but such equipment is available in Columbia, and money can buy the equipment and operators."

"In a nutshell here is the over all plan. We are going to put operators into the zone with the intention of infiltrating a ring that we think is the heart of an operation that plans to damage the canal so that it cannot be used for months or maybe years. I don't want to minimize the danger of such an operation. Now that I have given you a brief summary of what we plan to do, I cannot go into specifics until I have your sworn commitment that what I am about to tell you will go no farther than the three of you."

After a pause of a minute or so - "Betty do you get any idea of your part in this operation?"

"I'm going to the canal?"

"Yes! Would you like to think about it for a minute or so, or maybe until tomorrow?"

"No, I don't need any more time. If you feel I can do this job, then I am willing to serve. Let's go for it!"

"Great! You can do it!"

The Club Paradise is a nightclub in Panama City. It is considered the hot spot in town. We have reason to believe it is a front for the ring we are trying to penetrate. The owner and operator of the club is Carlos Alfonso, better know as the Bull. He is ruthless and very difficult to get to know. He has one weakness - blonde American women.

A band, with a singer, entertains at the club each night, and many of the guests are North American soldiers. There is a 7 p.m. curfew, for law abiding American soldiers, and local citizens. After the curfew begins, we believe enemy agents and the locals plan their work at the club. Alfonso needs a singer that can sing in English with his band. He has used mostly native singers, but about six months ago he did hire an American female singer. She got involved with one of the musicians and after a performance one night disappeared and has never been seen since. It is suspected that the Bull had her snuffed out. Since that time he hired another singer, but she is not very good and can be replaced. To be brief and to the point, "Betty, we want you to be the next singer at Club Paradise."

"Who me?"

"Yes. Betty, we want you to be the next singer at Club Paradise."

"At present the club is OFF LIMITS to American soldiers, but arrangements will be made to lift these
restrictions a couple of weeks before you arrive to
apply for a job."

"Any questions?"

"Yes I have one big one."

"Okay Betty let's have it!"

"How far will I have to go with this "great lover"?

"You will not have to do anything that you're uncomfortable with. The plan is to keep him interested and
craving more than he can have. He has a tremendous
ego and will do most anything to satisfy it. Mac and
David will be working at the club, so if you get into a
bad situation they'll be but a stone's throw away,
ready to rescue you."

"Wouldn't this blow my cover?"

"Yes, but if this meant saving you from a dangerous
situation it would have to be blown. We are not going
to sacrifice you Betty."

"Mac and David speak perfect Spanish. The club will
need a couple of waiters a week before you come on
the scene. "We have arranged for two of his waiters to
disappear."

"I have one problem."

"What is it Betty?"

"I am not a great singer. It is true that I have sung in
plays and the like, but a nightclub performer I am
not."

"Betty, you won't have to worry about quality, since
they will not be judging your voice - if you get my
drift."

"Well, I guess I'll have to start brushing up on the latest tunes on the hit parade."

"We will all meet in three days to finalize the plans. I can tell you that your first stop out of DC will be Biloxi, Mississippi where Keesler Field is located. Your medical records will be brought up to date by starting with a general physical for each of you. Remember, you are not to discuss what you've heard in this room with anyone - and I mean anyone."

Betty left the meeting in a somewhat dazed condition. Returning to her room she spent a considerable time thinking about the future ... it was all pretty scary. Were they desperate, or did they really believe she could pull off this dangerous job. So the FBI has no female agents - they had to ask me. Why? Do I have the looks and the singing talent to get the job done? I cannot turn back now. I have been bugging everyone about getting an assignment out of the country - and now I have one, but what an assignment.

The night was filled with doubts, fears, and unending questions. Sleep refused to come until just before dawn. Soon after she had just dropped off to sleep, Betty awakened suddenly with an amazing idea from nowhere - or was it her dreams?

'If they really need me badly enough, and Jack Krum said that was the case, then how about Mr. Krum doing me a favor. Tell me about the Alamo team and if Tony is a member.'

"Hello, may I speak to Mr. Krum?"

"May I ask who is calling?"

"Yes, my name is Betty Peterson."

"Just a moment please."

"Well hello Betty, what can I do for you?"

"Mr. Krum I would like to come to your office and talk with you for a few minutes."

"Sure, come on over."

"Thank you, I'll be right there."

Betty opened the door to Mr. Krum's office to be greeted by his secretary. "Are you Miss Peterson?"

"Yes I am."

"Please come with me."

While the secretary lightly knocked on another door, swinging it open without hesitation, a voice from within called, "Come on in Betty, good to see you."

Betty was extremely tense and anxious, and being aware that a telephone call received can kill concentration and thought processes, she quickly began stating her case.

"Mr. Krum", "Please Betty, Jack is my name."

Betty took a deep breath, moistened her lips and started again.

"Jack, it's like this. I have a friend who is also in the OSS. I believe he is on a very special assignment - operation Alamo. I haven't heard from him for months and I don't know where he is and I have been sick with worry wondering where and how he is. Can you help me?"

"How do you know he is assigned to Alamo?"

"I don't know for sure, but he fits the description of one of the members of the team, and I know that at one time this team was in training at the Virginia camp."

"Betty, you know the policy on such matters. To give out such information might jeopardize the safety of the team and in turn result in a failed mission."

Betty had gotten past her apprehensions and was determined to go head to head with the OSS.

"I know all about policy, but I am asking you for a special favor. I need to know where he is, and if he is still alive before I go on this mission."

Jack could see the strain in Betty's face as she pled with him, and immediately became concerned that such a distraction could put her in personal jeopardy.

"Betty you must get this out of your mind and think about your own mission. If I hear anything about such a mission - which I am sure I won't - I will pass it along to you. By the way who is this lucky stiff?"

"His name is Tony De Angelo."

Betty left Jack Krum's office without any assurance of finding out about Tony or his whereabouts. All she had to hang on to was hope, and that seemed very remote now.

A couple of days had passed with no word of Tony or the trip. Finally the team received their orders: Fly to Keesler Field in Biloxi, Mississippi. As she made preparation to leave, Betty felt surely she would get some response from Mr. Krum before she left. At least he could say he had tried. As the plane pulled away from the ramp she contemplated the situation, 'Just shows how unconcerned they really are - these OSS people. I wish now that I had refused this mission.'

Biloxi was a nice little city stretching along the beach on the Gulf of Mexico, however, the physical exam and the shots were not so pleasant. After a few days the team was informed that their next stop would be Miami, Florida. TOA would be 1300 the following day. Betty had still held out hope that Mr. Krum would call her. She was becoming increasingly bitter at the way she had been treated since entering the OSS; as though she were the enemy.

At 1030 she received an unidentified phone call:
"Betty, meet me at the lighthouse along the beach in fifteen minutes?"
"Who is this?"
"Be there in fifteen minutes." The phone clicked.
Betty thought that it sounded like Mr. Krum. 'What would he be doing in Biloxi, requesting me to meet him at a public place. She was still mumbling to herself as she quickly put on a jacket, grabbed her purse and headed out the door.

When she arrived at the lighthouse no one was anywhere to be found. She waited five, ten, fifteen minutes; then presumed someone was playing a joke on her - probably David; he was the jokester. As she started walking along the sea wall, a man dressed in grungy clothes, wearing a sun hat pulled down low on his head hiding most of his face, fell into step alongside of her.
"Betty, don't say anything, just listen."
Betty's heart started to pound because she was certain he was Mr. Krum, and she just knew he was going to tell her something about Tony. Would it be

good or bad? She felt a cold chill causing her body to shiver, even though the night was mild.

Speaking in a low voice as they walked along, he said, "Betty, Tony is on the Alamo team. He is in good condition as of two days ago. He is somewhere around Rome, Italy. Their mission completion date is unknown. I cannot tell you anymore. You must not mention this meeting to anyone - I mean not anyone." He finished sternly.

"Oh thank you Mr _ _ _ _." A hand quickly covered her mouth.

"Remember - - no one! Good luck on your mission."

The mysterious stranger walked on down the beach alone, and although he did not identify himself, Betty was positive it was Mr. Krum.

'Tony is alive and well. Now I can tackle my mission with a purpose - now I can look forward to a future with Tony.'

The flight to Miami was uneventful, but for Betty it was a time to reflect back to the good old days with Tony. She could still feel his last kiss with his arms wrapped tightly around her.

After a night of rest the team was called to a meeting with the OSS and FBI. It was now time to finalize plans for their mission. Mac and David would go to Panama before Betty. They would apply for, and get, jobs as waiters at the Club Paradise. The plan for Betty was a bit more complicated. She would need an exacting cover for being in Panama City. Her cover was laid out thusly:

She had been singing in and around Cleveland, Ohio

in small clubs. She had gotten in trouble with the mob, and in desperation joined the WACS to get away. She went to Fort Ogelthorpe, Georgia for basic training and was then assigned to the Corps of Engineers to work in the Canal Zone as a clerk. After a while she would decide she did not like the army - and its regulations - and go AWOL. She would desperately need a job, so she would approach Carlos for a singing job at the club.

"Will Carlos the Bull buy this story?" Asked one of the FBI agents.

"He will have to since it is the best cover story we can come up with." Replied one of the senior OSS agents. "If anyone can improve on this cover story please let us know about it. We will be more than happy to listen. Betty will be sent down with one of our army units. All her records will be there in the event they have her investigated at the club. We know the ring has people working for it, and they possibly would check her credentials. By the way Betty, you will be known as T/5 Mary McCullum. Your new identity will begin when you leave Miami. You will have a short hair cut for the army, and a blonde wig for your job at the club. Mac will be known as Luis. David will be Rafael. Any questions? If not we will meet at the quartermaster department tomorrow and get our clothing and other equipment. This is Wednesday; we will have a final meeting Saturday at 10:00 hours. This will be our last meeting together; it will be your last opportunity for questions and suggestions, so come prepared."

As the group broke up, David moved over to Betty.

"How about us going out on the town Thursday night? Maybe a farewell party."

"You mean you, Mac and I?"

"No I mean just you and me."

"David I appreciate your invitation but I would be a drip of a date."

"Oh, you mean I'm a dud?"

"No, you are a swell person, it's just a case of not being interested in getting involved with anyone - I have a steady."

"Oh, I didn't know. Who is the lucky fellow and why isn't he down here protecting his interests?"

"He is in the OSS on another assignment."

"Are you sure you don't want to go out for a break in the scenery?"

"I will go out with you and Mac as friends if you would like."

"Well, why not! Let's make it a date for 19:00 hour for Thursday night. Mac and I will pick you up and we'll start with dinner. I hear they have great seafood down here."

"That will be great - see you then."

The meeting at the quartermasters was uneventful other than the kaki uniform and dog tags Betty received. She was issued a uniform that at least half way fit. She had a barracks bag full of clothing, probably all as ill fitting. As she started to leave, Ed, one of the FBI agents that had been attending the meetings, walked out with her. As they started to go their separate ways, Ed caught Betty by the arm to detain her.

"By the way you, Mac and David are restricted to the base and are not to be seen anywhere around Miami. Too easy for someone to identify one of you later."

"I didn't know we were restricted."

"Well, just thought I would remind you."

As they parted company she wondered how he could have known they planned to go out that night. Had they bugged her room? Did they have them wired and they did not know about it? Would they do such a thing? Yes, they would! Her new shoes - were they wired? After examining each shoe, which outwardly showed no sign of a bug it proved nothing since one could be lodged inside the heels. No need to call David or Mac, she was sure they had been warned also. There was nothing for her to do but wait for Saturday morning. Well, she could spend this quiet time vocalizing and learning lyrics.

Saturday morning was greeted with oppressive heat characteristic of Florida in June, made tolerable only by the continuous ocean breezes. As the three gathered for their briefing, they were taken aback at the OSS and FBI representation. What a send off. Mac and David had let their beards grow the past few days, and were wearing deck clothes. Betty came as T/5 Mary McCullum of the WACS. They kidded back and forth as they checked out one another's disguise. "You know", said David, "I believe they came to see us do something out of the ordinary, like pull a rabbit out of a hat." "Yeah," added Mac, "kinda' like monkeys at the zoo, with people standing around watching them pick fleas."

Betty and Mac laughed, but they did feel self conscience; especially Betty with her short coiffed hair.
Presently there was a tap, tap on the rostrum.

"Okay, let's all simmer down and get to our seats."

There was the usual shuffling to get to the seats of
choice.

"We are here this morning to go over the details of
this operation. By the way, the mission's code name
is "Snow Cap."

"There are a couple of guests here today who have not
been in on the planning, nor the details, of this operation. For this reason I am going over them again."

The team had no way of knowing at the time, but one
of them was a high-ranking agent in the FBI. The
President wanted a firsthand account of this operation. The president's wife, and others who were pushing the cause of feminism, wanted to be kept up to
date. Why? Betty was the first female agent used by
the FBI and they all wanted her to succeed.

"I would like to introduce the three agents who will
play a major part in Snow Cap. The big guy on my left
is R. MacLaughlin, code name Luis, from the FBI. The
handsome one, though not as large, is David Sears
from the FBI, known as Rafael. The third member of
the team is Betty Peterson, known as T/5 Mary
McCullum, from the OSS, need I say more.

Mac and David will leave Miami by air on Sunday
at 0900 hours for the Island of Jamaica. They will
land at Kingston where jobs have been prearranged
on a Panamanian freighter loaded with bauxite headed for the west coast. When they arrive in Panama

they will jump ship and fade into the civilian population then turn up at the Club Paradise where they will be hired as waiters. The details of this employment have already been discussed and finalized.

Betty will fly out of Miami for the naval base at Guantanamo, Cuba. From there she will fly to the base at the Panama Canal where she will be assigned to the U.S. Army Engineers. We're allowing from two to three weeks for all the maneuvering to transpire, thereby allowing the team to get in position at the Club Paradise. Any questions."

"Will there be any suspicions about a WAC showing up at the Canal?"

"No. We have sent several down there already so there should be no suspicion when another one arrives. When T/5 Mary McCullum leaves the army and applies for a job at Club Paradise her name will be Jo Dutton. Are there any questions or comments? If not the meeting is adjourned. "

After the meeting the number two man from the FBI, and a couple of his associates, just had to make personal contact with Betty.

"Young lady I just wanted you to know the FBI is very grateful for your service to your country, and in particular to the FBI. You know we men are not equipped for such a job."

"Thank you very much." Betty graciously replied.

"You know if all the women are as pretty as you in the OSS, I might just put in for a transfer." They all laughed, and agreed.

Betty was somewhat embarrassed.

"We'll be following your operation very closely and assure you that the FBI will back you up in every way."

"Thank you sir."

As they shook hands there was an obvious mutual admiration for one another.

As the passengers prepared to board, the scorching sun tended to accelerate the loading processes. None cared to remain beneath its searing rays longer than necessary. The DC-6 flight to Guantanamo Naval Base, on the island of Cuba, was quite bumpy and also hot. There were several military persons aboard but T/5 McCullum did not want to know them. As she thought about her mission, her palms would get sticky and her heart would skip a beat. 'What am I getting myself into? Can I really pull this caper off?' Such thoughts spun through her mind over and over again. Time was closing in as the plane reached the air base in Cuba. They would have their final briefing during the layover. As the plane landed and pulled up to the ramp, everyone began debarking. T/5 McCullum was met by a soldier who escorted her to a room off the lobby where she met with two OSS agents, and three from the FBI. During the meeting she was told to stay close to her quarters for a couple of days, after which she would be united with other military personnel, allowing her arrival to be as routine as possible. They checked her equipment, dog tags, and orders. She had to be one hundred percent military. Now there was nothing to do but wait!

TWENTY

Titus and Suez were the first to return to the little barn. Their report was anything but optimistic. Germans were very active, and as a result, the partisans were extremely cautious. They eagerly waited the return of other members of the team, trusting their report was an improvement over their own. By the tenth of June the entire team had returned to the little barn just outside Corie.

"What's been going on around here while we were gone?" Asked the Major.

"There was an air drop three nights ago about four miles southeast of Cisterna. Some food supplies, and money, but nothing of importance in the way of further instructions."

"Well," as the Major looked at the group, "let's get it all out on the table."

"Okay Major. We have some good news and bad news," replied Rick. "There are so many rumors going around that it's hard to even venture a guess as to what's fact or fiction. For example; the Allies are going to invade Italy; the Germans will be pulling out within ten days. These are just samples of what we've been hearing."

"Tony, how about the civilian population?"

"I was shocked to find so many of the people that my family knew when we left Italy had either died or moved away. Some went into the army and some have been jailed. The civilians around here are scared to death. Many have been turned over to the Gestapo or Italian Police for rewards. We stayed with an uncle that I knew I could trust above everyone else. He said things were very bad and that food was a major issue. Many people are so desperate they're willing to do anything for food. The problem with trusting hungry people is when they are fed they tend to have a different attitude. They might tell the truth to get food then forget what they said once they're hunger is satisfied."

"Captain James how do you assess the situation?"

"I think Tony is absolutely correct with his assessment. With the exception of his uncle and one or two of his relatives, I feel that there is little, if any, help we can get from the civilian population. They're afraid to help, and if they did agreed to assist us, they could become undependable in threatening circumstances. I can only say this based on what I saw and heard, we are strictly on our own. The less contact we have with civilians the safer we will be."

"Mario and I have been in Rome visiting the partisans, even out in the suburbs. The Germans are cracking down on them more each day and many of those who were able to help even three months ago are no longer available. Those that remain are too frightened to offer much assistance. There is much unrest even among the political leaders, and fear has become paramount on both sides because of the unknown. Because of this, our mission is going to be very difficult to accomplish. Since there have been several attempts on the life of our target, he is making less and less public appearances. Our target is becoming more paranoid each day. His position and power seem to be sorely dependent on the Germans. He has a pitiful few in his inner circle that he can really trust. "

"Can we possibly get someone on the inside to do the job?" asked Captain James.

"It appears to me that this would be the best approach - as of right now." replied Cooper.

"What do you think about the situation, Mario?"

"We know that our target is a very vain and egotistical person. He is driven by his desire to have people think he is equal to any Caesar who has ever lived. He has had many pet projects during his career, but none that he has prized more than those around Cisterna and Anzio - the draining of the Pontine Marshes. This feat created such towns as Aprilia, Littoria, and, of course, the Mussolini Canal, which drains the area. Probably his most esteemed creation would be the settlement of Aprilia. Aprilia was a compact, geometrically laid out, cluster of three and four story brick buildings designed in 1936, and completed in 1938 to serve as a model for Fascist farm settlements. 1943 will mark the fifth year of the completion. It is rumored that our target may very well visit this town to mark the fifth anniversary."

"Are you saying this might be our one and only opportunity?"

"I don't know if it will happen, but if it does, we would have a better chance to accomplish our objective than trying to move into the inner circle. There could be several opportunities along the way for some good shots, or possibly on a narrow street where we could toss in a couple of grenades."

"When do you think this event will take place, Mario?"

"The best information we have regarding this potential visit is around July 11th."

"What do you think about this, Major - is it reliable?"

"Mario has some good connections. We will try to get more confirmed information, but for the time being it's the best we have. For the present we can make this D-day with options. We'll start planning this date for the hit. What do you men think about the plan so far?"

All nodded in agreement.

Major Cooper stood eyeing the group.

"We have about a month to get ready and that is really cutting it short, but we have no choice."

"Mario, what about you and Tony going back to Rome to try and confirm this date. If the date and event is still on, then you can go by Aprilia on your way back here and see if we can get any help from the locals there. The rest of the team will check out the terrain and select a possible location for the hit. Let's plan to meet back here in one week - say, June 17th."

"If we decide on Aprilia as the place for the hit - or the near proximity - we will have to be established in the area with a legitimate reason for being there. Any questions? If not, good luck and good hunting."

The distance from the barn to Aprilia was just about sixteen miles, as the crow flies. A railroad runs through the area from Rome, circles the hills west of Albana through the town of Ceochino, Osteriaccia, on by Campaleone and Campaleone station about two miles to the south, then through Carroceto, (a hamlet 500 yards to the southwest of Aprilia), ending at the town of Anzio and the beach. The area was on the edge of many gullies and ravines to the west of Aprilia. It would be possible for the team to hide in one or more of these gullies for a night or two. There were two houses close to the road, and the railroad, that might be useable; if the occupants agreed.

"What do you think about the possibility of taking over one of those houses - maybe putting the occupants under house arrest?"

After a pause, Captain James spoke almost in a whisper.

"That might be the safest move on our part, but what if a relative, or neighbor, dropped in for a visit?"

"We could lock them up with the others" shot back Joseph.

"Cooper", with a broad grin on his face, "have you ever tried to hold an Italian woman against her will?"

The endless days drug relentlessly as the team waited for Mario and Tony to return from their mission to Rome. They stayed on lookout all day and into the night, but still there was no sign of them. The greatest concern was for their safety. Finally someone braved the question audibly. "Do you suppose Tony and Mario have been taken prisoners?"

"I don't want us to think that way" answered the calm reassuring voice of Major Cooper. "They are smart and will not take any chances. They might have had to lay over along the way back."

That was a good answer, but still there was that possibility of being captured, especially in Rome.

After a delay of two days and two nights, Tony and Mario finally returned to the barn. With a rush of excitement and cheerful greetings; the obvious questions were tumbling out; "What took you so long? Why were you so late getting back here?" "You really had us worried, and deeply concerned," the Major added.

"We are sorry Rick, but we had to lay low two different times because of road blocks. Then in Rome they were searching a section at a time looking for anyone that might be on their list. The people in Rome are in panic. The Germans are expecting the Italian mainland to be invaded some time during the summer. They're tightening the screws on everyone. But we made it back without a hitch, didn't we Tony?"

"Yeah, we made it back, but not without sweating off some pounds. This guy would not let me eat while we were hiding. He said the smell of food could be detected by the Germans."

"I know you both are bushed and need some sleep. Hit the sack and when you wake up we will hear your report."

"Don't mind if we do, Major."

The sun broke over the Lepini mountain range to the southeast to begin a beautiful summer day. Rain had fallen during the night leaving the fresh smell of rain. The clean fresh look of the foliage reminded Tony of a time he and Betty visited Overton Park for a picnic after a summer rain. They laughed because there were no dry places to spread their food, so they just sat down on the wet grass and got soaked from the bottom up. Such thoughts are not good when one is about to take part in a very hazardous mission. It is hard to think beyond a point in time that might just be the end. How he would love to be back in the little café working along side Betty every day. 'Guess she has forgotten all about me - maybe that is the way it should be.'

Tony's thoughts were interrupted when he felt a hand on his shoulder,

"Ready to meet the board, Tony?"

"Yeah, ready as ever."

"Before you fellows start your report here is a special breakfast. Two fresh eggs from the barn, English crumpets, and a cup of English tea."

Tony had tried to eat English food before, and just couldn't resist - "how can one call crumpets and tea, food?" he said with a chuckle, as he began to eat.

"You tell 'em," chimed in Rick.

"Now that Tony and Mario have had a good rest, and a delicious English breakfast, they should be in top shape to fill us in on their trip to Rome. Mario why don't you go first."

"Very well, I'll give you what I have, then Tony can fill in the blanks. I was able to see one of our partisans that I couldn't get to on my last trip. He filled me in on some important information. There is a move inside the inner circle of Il Duce to get rid of the Germans and sell out their "Leader." For this reason it is now easier to find out about the movements of our target. These people are in sympathy with us. They want no part of a hit, but they would be greatly relieved if it could be done by outsiders."

"You mean have their dirty laundry cleaned by those with guts."

"Yes, that's about it."

"Our target is coming to the celebration at Aprilia. The date as of now is July 18th. He will be coming by train from Rome to Corroceto and then by car to the town where there will be a parade, speeches, and of course a very short appearance of the "leader." His train will be heavily armed. The logical place for the hit would be after he leaves the train and motor's from the station to the place of celebration. When he speaks he will be behind a steel plated stand with only his head visible. The crowd will be pushed back twenty yards from the stage, ruling out the possibility of a grenade or firearm. Tony did I leave out any details?"

"One thought that was mentioned in Rome. Blow up the tracks and then attack the rail car."

"True, it was mentioned, but I would consider this an impossibility."

"Sounds to me like your idea of hitting him between the railroad station and the parade ground is the way we should go." Commented Captain James.

Mario shot a sober look in the direction of the major. "What do you think?"

"I say - go for it! It might be the only chance to reach our target out side of Rome."

There were looks passed around the group but no one voiced an objection.

The Major continued. "We will need to have a couple of men in Compoleone the day the train comes through to make sure our target is set up properly. Tony needs to get a job at the factory as a cover for our target date. With Tony a part of the population at Aprilia we can keep up with the activities and maybe have a clearer picture of how we can get the job done. Possibly a few days before July 18th , or the day of the celebration we can move into the caves just west of Corroceto.

"Tony, we'll have a couple of messengers for you to use, furnished by the partisans."

"How will I know them Major?"

"They will find you."

"No! I want to know who they are so that I can check them out before they know my identity."

"Okay we can work this out. As you know, the date and plans for this operation can be changed by the planners from several locations, so we will have to be in a position to adjust at the last minute. As of now the target hit is scheduled on July 18th around the town of Aprilia. May I caution each of you that our lives depend on our ability to blend with the locals. If our identity is suspected in the slightest, it could cause the authorities to become suspicious, and we know what could happen. Let's be extremely careful. Are there any questions?"

TWENTY - ONE

After weeks of waiting, T/5 Mary McCullum was ordered to the Panama Canal. While she had been eager to get on her way, now that the time had come, her racing heart had gone out of control, and her mouth was dry as cotton.

The waiting had better prepared her for the part she was expected to play at the club. She had been tutored in Spanish and could sing a couple of songs in the native tongue of Panama. She had also been practicing her typing and other clerical skills. 'Maybe more time would help; yet maybe it wouldn't. It's time to get on with the job.' She determined.

A jeep, driven by a young private, was sent to pick her up. Once the barracks bag was secured, they headed for the airport. At 0700 hours on June 20th , the DC-3 lifted off the field at Guantanamo, Cuba. Four hours later the plane was scheduled to land in Panama. There was an oddly mixed group of passengers on board. As usual there were the self acclaimed "lady killers" wanting to know all about her, and how to get in touch. She had to play the game and give them a little personal run down, and, how to get in touch with her later. She also had to give them a little encouragement, and leave the door open for a possible date in the future. 'If they really knew that I was an agent of the OSS, they might not be so eager to get to know me.' She mused.

After settling down for the bumpy hot ride - it was time for a nap or to just close her eyes and daydream. 'I wonder what Tony is doing and where he is? What if David and Mac did not get into the club? What if they don't accept me at the club, then what? I wonder if I should be back in school at Vandy?' Betty sat motionless until sleep overtook her anxiety. A sudden thumping, then bumping sound jolted her back to reality some hours later.

She sat up quickly thinking the plane had hit something.

"What's happening?" She asked a young lieutenant.

"Nothing, that was the landing gear locking in place. We are going in for a landing - we are in Panama." The landing was pretty rough. As the plane taxied to the terminal, one of the crew yelled.

"Get your gear and head for the door!"

A truck was waiting to carry the six Army personnel to the base. The ride gave them a bird's eye view of the city. Dirty, full of unattended children, and of course, pimps waiting at every stop the truck made. The U.S. Government had done a lot to improve living conditions in parts of the city by installing gutters and a water system. Particular sections of Panama City never change. A squalid condition existed in much of the surrounding areas of the city. Panama

City had clubs of all descriptions. There were the cheap movie houses showing pictures that were off limits for the U.S. military. Each theatre was well covered with native prostitutes at the exit doors. Venereal disease was all too common among them. The military warned of the high risk, and the consequences, of having sex with these women. Most heeded, but there was always a group that did not.

T/5 Mary McCullum was assigned to Fort Claxton five miles north of Panama City. After checking into the personnel office, she was assigned to her barracks; followed by unpacking and bed making. She was not due to report until the next morning, so it was a good time to catch up on her sleep. Since there were only five WAC's assigned to this station, they were living in the nurses quarters.

The office was smaller than Mary had imagined. She was replacing a sergeant being sent to the ETO. Her immediate boss, a Tech/Sergeant from Minnesota, was not in the least sympathetic, nor pleased, at having to supervise a woman. "Women have no business in this man's army, and I'm not about to help them pass the test." He repeated this attitude on many occasions.

The army life was quite different from any experience Mary had been exposed to since she came into the OSS. The work was uncomplicated and routine. She had made good friends with one of the nurses, Lieutenant Margaret Williams from Oxford, Mississippi. They discovered they had a lot in common since they were both from the south.

Mary had not been contacted by anyone from the FBI. It had not been confirmed that Mac (Luis) and David (Rafael) had been established at the club as waiters. Until she was contacted she would play it safe and stay close to work and her quarters.

One day she received an unexpected phone call. "Come to the motor pool at 17:30. Stay at the gate until you are asked if you need a lift to "Mama's." 'Was this a joke?' She asked herself, 'or was this the contact she had been waiting for?'

T/5 McCullum left the office and headed for the motor pool arriving at exactly 17:30. As vehicles passed back and forth through the gate she drew a lot of whistles and cat calls, but no one offering to give her a lift to Mama's. Suddenly the same drifter that had just gone into the motor pool came back and stopped.

"How about a ride to Mama's?"

Mary looked at the jeep driver - 'why this person is only a driver, surely my contact would be someone of importance, wouldn't he?'

"Sure." She replied.

"Hop in," he said grinning.

"You got a name?" He continued.

"T/5 Mary McCullum."

"No; I know what your name is now. What was it in Washington?"

"Oh, it was Flicker." She answered lightly.

"May I introduce myself, I am Charley Wells of the FBI."

"Well, I am glad someone finally decided to admit that

I was still on the payroll."

"McCullum we will meet when necessary. Being a driver gives me freedom in the area. Mama's is the name of a meeting place in the future. It will be another two weeks or more before we plan for you to go over the hill. Luis and Rafael are in place at the club. The club has been opened for our military men, beginning this week. In the meantime play your part at the base. Complain about harassment, your work, and in general, your dissatisfaction with the terrible conditions down here. Next week you can have a confrontation with one of the officers and get put on report for insubordination.

"Will they put me in the brig?"

"No! Don't go that far - just far enough to get extra duty. In general McCullum, you are to be a very unhappy broad who's fed up with the army."

"I understand you have made friends with the nurse, Lt. Williams, that's good. Cultivate this friendship. Go into town with her, visit Club Paradise; you might even make a pass at the bartender working there. Set yourself up as a flirt."

"Is Margaret an agent?"

"No, she is just what she appears, an army nurse."

"That's good."

"Why don't you plan to go into town this weekend. The next weekend you should be restricted to the base because of your insubordination."

T/5 McCullum and Lt. Williams made their way through the crowded streets of Panama City. For the first time they were able to see first hand the natives of Panama City and the behavior of a city without restraints. They drifted in and out of the souvenir shops, jewelry stores, etc., just casually taking in the local color.

Mary felt bad about using Margaret, but also felt she would understand if she knew the reason.

Mary nonchalantly said, "Let's make one of the clubs before curfew."

"It's okay with me Mary, which one?"

"There's one club I've heard a lot about at the base - I think it's - a - a - Club Paradise. Yeah, that's it." Mary played it real cool to avoid arousing suspicion.

"I don't know where it is, but maybe our cab driver will know how to get there." The driver knew the address, but the problem was whether the cab could make it that far. It must have been a 1920 model.

Club Paradise was the typical nightclub. There were the standard chairs, tables, bar and a small dance floor, fronted by a platform for the band. Mary spotted Rafael but was careful to show no sign of recognition.

The headwaiter approached them asking, "Would you ladies like a table?"

"No, we'll just sit at the bar, thank you."

As they moved from one section of the club to another, Mary was giving the males a quick once over. If Charley wanted her to be friendly with one of the employees, she at least wanted one that was half way attractive. The bartender was no Adonis, but not bad to look at either. Mary quickly caught his eye, and as he handed her a drink she let her fingers linger on his for just a second. That was all it took to get him into the game. "I get off in another hour. How about you and me going out on the town - maybe visit one of the better clubs."

Mary responded with a smile and a flash of her blue eyes. She didn't want to come on too strong, yet she wanted to indicate that she could be persuaded. Luis had casually moved to the bar on the pretense of talking to Margaret. He had no idea of Mary's plans, but hoped she could give him a subtle hint of her next move. Mary made eye contact with Luis as she replied to the bartender,

"I'm so sorry - can't today, but we'll be back in a week or two, then perhaps you can show me the town."

Luis nodded slightly at Mary to let her know he understood her timetable.

The band was about what Mary expected; a lot of Latin music, with a few American tunes thrown in. The female singer was as mediocre as the band. Even with reservations about her singing, Mary felt she was an improvement over that girl, and maybe her looks could do the rest.

As the days passed, Mary and Margaret had become quite close friends. Mary really felt wretched betraying Margaret's friendship, because naturally she would not understand her forthcoming radical behavior. Maybe sometime after this whole affair had ended she could sit down with her and explain this unusual episode in her life.

On Wednesday morning she decided to start her campaign of rebellion. One of the sergeants pitched some papers on her desk.

"I want those finished immediately!" He barked.

"I will when I get time," replied T/5 McCullum.

"What did you say?"

"I said I would do your work when I get time - you heard me. I know you're not deaf!"

The sergeant turned red in the face, did an about face and headed for the lieutenant's office.

T/5 McCullum expected the lieutenant to react, but for the remainder of the day he didn't say a word. The next morning the lieutenant came to her with some special work.

"Corporal McCullum I want this work completed and in my office by noon."

"I doubt that I can complete it by noon, sir. It will probably be some time this afternoon, or maybe in the morning."

"Corporal, do you know who you are talking to?"

"Sure, a lieutenant."

"You had better have that report finished and on my desk by noon or else!"

After the lieutenant walked away, McCullum had some choice words that she spoke to herself loud enough to be heard by a few people who were close by.

'Who does he think he is, General Marshall?'

True to T/5 McCullum's word the report was not ready by noon.

True to the lieutenant's word, he backed up his threat by having her sent to the captain's office.

"Did you send for me sir?"

"I certainly did, and you may not stand at ease!"

The captain gave her the once over before lighting into her.

"Perhaps you haven't gotten it straight in your empty head young lady, but this is the army. When a superior officer tells you to do something you had better jump! You are not working for the Prudential Life Insurance Company, or some ladies dress shop." The Captain's face was extremely red and Mary was concerned that he might explode.

"Do you understand?" He growled.

"Yes sir, I do understand. I have my own work to do and felt it more important to finish mine before I started on Lieutenant Johnson's."

The Captain continued, rising nearly half out of his chair.

"That is another problem you seem to have. You are not to think, you are to do what you are told to do and that's the way it's going to be around here - got it?"

Mary paused - "I think so, sir."

"So that you might have some time to think over what I have said to you, you are restricted to the post for the weekend, and on duty in the OD's office."

After a long searing stare, the Captain sharply spoke. "You are dismissed!"

Mary wheeled out of the captain's office, stomped through the main office, and slammed a book on a vacant desk. She wanted to be noticed - and noticed she was.

"I have had enough of this male domination." She

vehemently declared.

Everyone around the office got the picture - T/5 McCullum was fit to be tied.

"Mary I don't want to infringe on your business, but you had better be careful, you could get into a lot of trouble."

"Thank you Martha, but I don't care. I don't have to take this kind of treatment from a shave tail. He didn't have to turn me in."

After things cooled down, Mary wondered if she had been convincing - she believed she had.

Pfc. Charley Wells of the FBI paid her a visit the following week.

"You did a good job of letting them know you do not like the army or anyone in it." Charley was laughing. "How are things going now?"

"Oh, fine. I haven't caused them any more trouble and I'm even calling everyone, including the Sergeant, sir." She replied.

"That's fine. About Tuesday or Wednesday of next week get a pass to leave the Fort. Don't say anymore about your dissatisfaction with the army. Leave the Fort by cab, and I'll follow. We have a man dressed as a female that will look like you from a distance. This person will be seen by the MPs trying to get on a ship out of Panama. This should give you the cover needed to stay in Panama. When you go to the Club, your appearance will be altered when you don a long blonde wig."

"What about some of the people I've been around, or close to - like Margaret. Don't you think they'll recognize me at the club?"

"If they do, just say they are mistaken, you have never been in the army and never expect to be. Lt. Williams is a good soldier, and if necessary we will get to her if she discovers your real identity. It's doubtful that any of the people you have been around would ever associate you with the club singer.

Monday morning found T/5 McCullum hard at work and unusually cooperative. Things were going smoothly by Tuesday, so she asked for a pass for Wednesday afternoon to go into town. She gave the Sergeant a big smile, and called him Sir. She knew better, but it always made him feel his importance, and fed his ego. It worked like a charm, and she got a pass for Wednesday afternoon.

As promised she received a call from Pfc. Wells.

"I was calling to see when the replacements would come in?"

"They will be in Wednesday at 1600."

Wells knew that was the day and time Mary would leave the Fort. On Wednesday Mary hailed a cab and headed for town. The cab driver, to her surprise, was an FBI agent also. He gave her a suitcase and carried her to a hotel close to the canal. The plan was simple.

T/5 McCullum would enter the hotel as a WAC, then a male agent, dressed as a woman, would shortly exit the front door as a WAC. The stand-in would head for the dock, and busily check with every MP along the way for directions, attracting attention as she made her way down the dock.

T/5 McCullum was transformed to Jo Dutton

after a quick change to a civilian form fitting dress, and long blonde wig. There was no reason for anyone to believe the two women that exited the hotel were not two different people. The driver of the cab (FBI agent) drove her to the Club Paradise. She carried one suitcase and a makeup bag. She was told to keep a couple of her WAC uniforms in the suitcase just in case someone checked it at the club.

Betty hoped the same bartender she had made a pass at was on duty - he was.

"Hi there, I'm Jo Dutton, a singer. I'm looking for a job."

Studying her for a few moments, suddenly he blurted out, "Hey, aren't you the WAC that was in here last week?"

"Yes, but hold it down, don't tell everybody in Panama City. I want to see the boss - what's his name?"

"Carlos Alfonso, but you won't get in to see him."

"What do you mean," asked Jo. "I want to talk to him about singing in his club. I am good, much better than that chick he has now."

"Yeah, well you first better start explaining to me how come you came in here a WAC last week, and now a classy civilian looking for a singing job this week."

"You don't have to know everything do you? Let's just say when I came in here before I was a member of the U.S. Army, but today I am a civilian."

Jo was unaware that the bartender had pressed a buzzer that customarily signaled Carlos of impending trouble. Carlos stepped out of his office, but stopped short when he saw Jo. He liked what he saw, but had a suspicious feeling about her. The bartender glanced across the club and caught Carlos' signal for her to come back later.

"Look Jo, or whatever your name really is, you will have to come back tomorrow or the next day, Carlos isn't in today."

"Okay I will be back tomorrow." She emphasized, "I desperately need a job. I ditched the army and now I don't have a dime coming in. Can't you put in a good word for me?" She pleaded softly.

Jo found her friend down the street waiting for her. He was not surprised that she did not get to see Carlos.

"You know Jo they will check you out first. They have friends at the Fort and if Carlos gets clearance on you, with proof that you are telling the truth, you have nothing to worry about."

The driver took her to a low class hotel to spend the night. She no doubt was being watched.

"Jo, I have a room in the hotel tonight too, just in case. If I cannot get to you in time of trouble here is a .45 caliber pistol that you can tuck under your pillow. None of the men working for Carlos will bother you, but some of the natives might. You have the right to shoot anyone who enters your room uninvited."

The room was dingy, and the bed hard and lumpy, but otherwise the night was without incident. The next day Jo went back to the club. She got the same put off as the day before.

"Come back tomorrow."

She told her driver what had happened.

"That's normal Jo, they've been checking the Fort to see if you really were a WAC, and if you really did go over the hill."

"Do you think they believe me now?" She asked.

"That's a funny thing. Would you believe the people in your office didn't know you were missing the first day you were gone? They know it now, and I believe you will get your long awaited interview with the "Bull" tomorrow."

Around noon Jo made her way back to Club Paradise via her friendly taxi driver. This time she was escorted back to Carlos Alfonso's office. He was seated behind a desk in a swivel chair that was worn from too much use. He looked like the typical native; overweight, thin black mustache, and heavy black hair plastered down with too much grease. Looking at her with black beady eyes and a half smirk on his face, he said.

"So, you claim to be a singer better than my regular girl, and how come you went AWOL?"

Jo felt like a choice piece of steak in a butcher shop about to be devoured by a starving customer.

She looked him straight in the eyes. "I can sing, and I need a job."

"Well that was short and straight to the point. Tell me a little bit about yourself before you came to Panama. You must have a past history?

"I grew up in Toledo, Ohio and majored in drama in high school. After graduation I enrolled in drama and singing classes. It was there that I met a man who promised to promote my career. He got me small parts in off beat places. I did not know at the time that he was in the rackets - a collector. He crossed the mob and one night he didn't come home. A friend of mine told me he had been killed and that I had better make sure I was not in on the take. I knew nothing about his activities, but the mob wouldn't believe me. I was scared so I went to Cleveland, Ohio to hide out. Several weeks passed without an attempt to contact me, so I decided I was in the clear. I worked at a few small cafés and finally I got a job at the Breeze Club in downtown Cleveland. Street address is 1410 Elm and the phone number is 426345. A Mr. Eddie is the manager - ask for him."

This was the only lead the OSS gave Jo. They felt that this would be enough to convince Carlos if he wanted to check. The OSS was running the club and Mr. Eddie was an agent.

She continued, "I was doing okay at the club when I was told that one of my duties was to entertain some of the important customers in a special way. I told Mr. Eddie that I did not mind going out to dinner and dancing with special customers, but they made it clear that that was not all they wanted me to do. When I objected they told me that I had no choice. The word got around about my opposition to the rules of the club. A friend of mine, who took a risk, told me that there was another girl working there before me that would not comply. They found her body lying along the curb, it had been run over by a hit and run driver. "There's no getting' out honey," she said to me, "just play the game; it won't be too bad. I've been here for three years, and you know, once in a while you hit it lucky and meet some rich guys who tip big for good service."

Carlos was looking at her with sympathetic eyes that reflected belief.

She was wound up now, so she continued spinning her yarn. "I was in a corner. I knew that I couldn't go anywhere else and get a job without being found, but there was one way I knew I could escape - join the army. They would never find me there and even if they did I could not go back to the club. Anyhow, I enlisted in the WACs and was sent to Fort Oglethorpe, Georgia. After basic training I was assigned to the Corps of Engineers and later sent to the Panama Canal Zone. It didn't take me long to find that army life isn't for me. So, here I am."

By the time she finished her soliloquy, her body was quivering all over. 'Boy, I wonder if I convinced him?'

"Why don't you relax, take a fifteen minute break, then come to the platform and let us hear you sing."

Jo asked that only the piano accompany her for the audition.

She sang "Besame Mucho" in Spanish, and "As Time Goes By" in English.

As she sang "As Time Goes By" she could tell that Carlos was hooked.

"Okay Jo, consider yourself hired. Your pay will be determined by the crowd you draw into the club to dance and sit at the tables buying drinks."

"What about a place to stay? I've been staying at one

of the hotels, but I am afraid I might be recognized by an MP."

"Okay, you can have a room in the back of the club for a while - at least until the heat if off."

So far the plan seemed to be working. Staying in the club all the time would give her ample time to observe who came in after hours. It would also put her in an awkward position with Carlos, but with Luis and Rafael working the tables nearby, they would be close to give her assistance. However, Luis and Rafael were not permitted to stay in the club after closing.

Rafael was a proficient sketch artist, and was requested to extend his talent to expedite the identification of the ring members. Because Jo had gained entrance to the club after hours, she had been instructed to study the faces of men she noticed in the club after closing, then relay an accurate description for Rafael to portray on paper. Once these unknown men could be identified the sooner the FBI could close in on the ring. No doubt some of the natives had been helping the enemy agents, unaware of their mission. Some of these local gangs dealt in narcotics, prostitution, etc. It would be easy for foreign agents to integrate into a local group for cover. Her job for the moment would be to identify only the foreign agents.

Jo became a big draw at the club. She added class and atmosphere with her striking appearance, and smooth deliverance of a song. During the day the club was no longer off limits to American GIs. Soon GIs would purposely drop in just to hear current

North American tunes. They never got their fill, and affectionately referred to her as a piece of the "states."

At night the club's patrons were primarily Spanish, however the tunes she sang in English were just as well received.

For the first couple of nights nothing occurred after closing hours that Jo could identify as unusual. But the third night was quite different. Sometime after 2 a.m., just after the club had closed, she heard loud voices and what she thought was a scuffle. Things quieted down and she went back to sleep only to be awakened around 5 a.m. by screams, followed by the sound of gunshots: preceded by screams. Obviously she did not go back to sleep for the remainder of the night. She was scared, and felt extremely uncomfortable at what she heard.

The club opened at the usual time the next day. Nothing was said about the unusual disturbance of the past night, it was business as usual. The customary number of American GIs were on hand, and the band, with its normal off key presentations, was unchanged.

The first indication that things were not right was when she caught the eyes of Rafael across the room. He wore a very worried look on his face and indicated to Jo that he wanted to talk to her. As Jo completed her last number she moved toward their pre-arranged meeting place. He did not speak audibly, but handed her a very small piece of paper that read; 'Luis is missing, chew and swallow this note.'

This news hit Jo like a lightening bolt. Her mind

raced back to the event of the past night. Could the screams have come from Luis? Had they found out about him? Do they know about she and Rafael? All these thoughts spun through her mind as she began to shake. She hurried into the ladies rest room where she chewed up the note and washed it down with water. She was scheduled to sing again in a few minutes - but how could she? She knew her voice would quiver and knees knock. She was certain her shaken condition would be detected. What could she and Rafael do? There was no place to run to. Furthermore, to run would certainly give the mission away and may cause the deaths of others.

In an effort to get herself under control, she stiffened her back, threw back her shoulders, then looking at herself in the mirror said, "Jo, you wanted to be an OSS agent and get in on the big time spy stuff, well that's exactly where you are." She resolved in her heart, that for the sake of Rafael, and others involved in this mission, she would have to play her part out to the end - whatever the end. She determined in her mind that even if the end is tonight or next week, she must go out there and act as though nothing unusual had happened; just play it cool. As she turned away, her heart was deeply saddened as she remembered poor Luis ... he had already met his end.

TWENTY - TWO

The FBI and the OSS had concluded their investigation of the mysterious crash of the plane carrying Colonel Mayhew, who was on his way to
Casablanca to join the Alamo team. After a visual
study of some of the recovered parts from the DC-6 it
was concluded that some type of explosive device
destroyed the plane. After tests were made on parts
of the plane, it was further determined that the
explosive was TNT. Since it was now evident that this
crash was no accident, but sabotage, additional
investigation was underway to discover how the
explosives could have been put on the plane, and
when? After reviewing a list of possible candidates, it
revealed one name that could have had access to the
plane, other than those on board, after the ground
crew had left the plane - a member of the OSS
assigned to a top-secret mission.

Two FBI agents arrived at the office of the OSS
section chief in charge of the Alamo operation. The
Chief's name was Mantis - nick named "Big Man"
because of his stature. He was visibly irritated that the
two agents came to his office without an appointment.

"What do you men want?" He asked in a sarcastic tone.

One of the agents replied in a calm but direct manner, "I am afraid we have some alarming news."

"Well, what is it?"

As the two FBI agents began to present their findings about the downed plane, Mantis paid little attention to what was being said as he arrogantly puffed on a cigar, blowing smoke toward the ceiling as though bored.

"I know the plane was blown up, so get to the point." Mantis snorted.

"Well Sir, it is certain that one of your men planted the explosives on the plane that caused it to crash, killing Colonel Mayhew and twelve others."

"Well, who was it?"

"Agent Joseph Golden, code name Kite."

Mantis stood abruptly, glared at the agents and demanded.

"Are you sure?"

"Yes sir, we have unmistakable proof that he was the one who planted the explosives."

"We also have proof that this man is not an American citizen. He had been in the states for only a short time - since 1938."

"Well," replied Mantis, "it's not uncommon for such people to be used by the OSS."

"We understand that, but this man came out of Germany under some strange circumstances, and we now believe he was planted here to be used as an enemy agent in the future."

Mantis sat up in his large chair and looked intently at the two agents for some time without speaking.

One of the FBI agents broke the silence.

"Do you know where this man is?"

"Yes, I know where he is, but his location is secret. He is on a top secret mission overseas."

"This is very distressing news. This will cause us a great deal of problems - you have no idea!"

Mantis stood up, looked directly at the FBI agents.

"I thank you gentlemen for your work and for informing me as soon as you could. It will be up to the OSS from now on to clear up this matter. Please keep this matter confidential."

As the agents started to leave the office, Mantis walked a few steps toward the door - then turning toward the agents, "By the way, have you informed anyone in the OSS other than myself about this matter?"

"No, but we will file a written report to the front office of your organization today."

"That won't be necessary, I can do that." Replied Mantis in a more agreeable tone than previously displayed.

"Sorry sir, but we have to file this report - you know regulations."

The agents walked out of the office, closing the door and leaving Mantis to his thoughts.

The FBI had confirmed that the plane was sabotaged - but they had not been able to answer the big question - why? Did Colonel Mayhew know that a plot was underway to get rid of him because he knew some-

thing that he shouldn't? Had he made a discovery
while en route from Washington to Miami? Was he
being sent out of the country because he knew too
much? There were many unanswered questions at
this stage of the investigation. The FBI had been
around too long to accept a theory that the plane was
blown up for no apparent reason. The investigation
would continue until all the pieces of the puzzle were
in place.

Mantis sat in his chair for a long while thinking
about the FBI agents' visit. He would have to take
action; the information could not be suppressed.
Pushing the button on the intercom, he spoke, "Miss
Avent, will you get the chief on the phone and ask
him if he has time to see me now- it's very important."
"Yes sir, I will."
Moments later his secretary buzzed back saying,
"Sir, the chief said to come right over."
Mantis was ushered into the chief's office upon his
arrival.
"Sit down Mantis. Have a cigar and tell me why the
urgency of this visit."
It was not until after cigars had been lit, and each
had enjoyed the first puff, that Mantis spoke.
He carefully laid out the charges the FBI had made in
regard to agent Kite. (Joseph Golden).
The chief was shocked! "How could this be? Didn't
you pick these men for this assignment?"
"Yes sir, I did. In some slick manner this man slipped
through our screening."
"Do you believe him to be a German agent?"

"I am afraid he is. I don't know what he would gain on this mission unless he is after the names of our agents operating in Italy. I don't see how he could impede or stop the mission he is on now."

The chief blew smoke toward the ceiling.

"You know this man has got to be eliminated as soon as possible. The men with him are in grave danger, as well as the success of the operation."

After a long look at the chief, "Yes I know." Mantis agreed.

Rolling his cigar around in his fingers as though studying it, the chief said, "Since we do not know the real mission of this mole, it is of great urgency that he be eliminated without any delay. How soon can you lay out a plan - by tomorrow?"

"I will do my best chief. I feel that sending an agent from the states would take too long. I would like enough time to try to work through MI-6. That would be much faster if it could be worked out."

"All right, but do it quickly. Let me hear from you in twenty four hours."

"Yes sir."

At 0300 hours, Washington time, Mantis had a message sent to a contact in MI-6 in London in cryptic code: "There are moles in operation Alamo. They must be eliminated. Only Joseph Golden (a Jew), code name Kite, is clean. Please give completion date immediately. Urgent."

The time was 10:00 hours when the message reached London. At 11:30 the same day a reply was received in the office of the OSS in Washington, DC: "The

Texas crop will be gathered within a week."

Mantis hurried at once to the office of the Chief where he was ushered in without delay.

"Chief, I have had success in getting a member of MI-6 to take care of the job we discussed. They feel it can be accomplished within a week."

"Good! Good work Mantis."

Mantis hurried on, "This agent is very familiar with the terrain and should have little difficulty locating the team. He will be dropped into the area around Lettoria, and will report to us as soon as the assignment has been completed."

TWENTY - THREE

Tony had no difficulty securing a job in Aprilia as a maintenance man. Such a job gave him access to many areas that would enable him to observe the mainstream. Some of his relatives had recognized him and wanted to know why he was back in Italy. He could only tell them he was on a secret mission to help free Italy. It was risky to be recognized, but that was the only card he had to play. If he didn't stay too long in Aprilia there probably wouldn't be any questions from the authorities. Tony was to be the contact for the partisans in Rome who could hopefully furnish a reliable schedule for Nero. As late as July 10th the trip was still on, but it was considered wise to move into a wadi (gully) west of Aprilia.

The team consisted of Impala (Tony), Kite (Joseph), Falcon (Rick), Robin (Capt. James), Titus (Mario Berti), Suez (Major John Cooper). On the morning of July 11th, Suez received a radio transmission from London informing him of the arrival of an agent from MI-6. No reason was given. The agent arrived at the barn on July 14th. He introduced himself as Major Greene from MI-6. They were instructed to bring him up to date on the final plans of Alamo, and in return offer any suggestions he might have to improve the operation.

Major Greene was introduced to each member of the team present. At the time no one thought too much about it, but he was very attentive when Joseph was introduced, remarking as he shook hands, "I believe you are a Jew, are you not Kite?"

"Well, yes sir, and I am proud of it."

"Certainly, you should be."

Major Cooper had some reservations about the new-comer. Such an appearance was somewhat unusual, he thought, although his credentials were in order. He had never heard of this officer, and he had been in MI-6 for sometime. Major Greene informed Suez that he would like to meet with the entire group by 19:00.

At 16:20 hours Suez received a chilling message. "German agent in your area."

He showed the message to Titus.

"What do you make of this?"

Titus turned pale and began to look around as though looking for the German agent.

"Do you suppose this is the reason for the major from MI-6 to make this unexplained visit?"

"You know that just might be it. But why have we not been told before, and who sent the message?"

The entire team had assembled at the barn promptly at 19:00 hours. Although Major Greene asked for the overall plans, he didn't really seem to be that interested, Tony observed.

After a short input from each member, Major Greene announced that he and his driver would be returning to Rome that night. They dressed in Italian army uniforms, and along with proper passes, shouldn't have any trouble making the trip. Major Greene made it quite clear that the team was to remain in the barn until they heard from him.

"The roads to Cisterna are well covered with road blocks. Since it will be a moonless night, Kite, I want you to ride along with us as far as Cori, since you're familiar with the roads."

After the Major and Kite left, Rick made this observation,

"Boy, the Major and Joseph really hit it off right away."

"Yeah," remarked Tony. "They sure did. Maybe they have a love affair going."

"You mean you think they might be queers?"

"Could be," replied Tony.

The candles were out and the team, one by one, drifted off to sleep. Tony had been having diarrhea problems, and after about a half hour of trying not to - he had to make a dash for the bushes. As Tony squatted down he heard noise around the other side of the barn, and thought maybe someone else had the same problem. He heard a voice sounding just like Joseph talking to someone. Then he heard the unmistakable click of pins being pulled from hand grenades. Without warning the little barn suddenly exploded. He could not believe his eyes. Had the Germans located the barn? He quickly jerked up his pants, and without thinking, started back toward the little barn, but stopped dead in his tracks when shots rang out from automatic weapons. Were the shots coming from members of the team? His one thought was to help them. Smoke and fire were rapidly consuming the remains of the barn. He thought he saw at least three men through the smoke and almost yelled out to them, but before he did he heard a voice that could not be denied. Joseph was asking someone, "Are they all dead?"

Tony could not believe what he had just witnessed. He felt sick; he wanted to throw up, but there was nothing left in his stomach. His hands were cold and clammy - his body was ice cold. Suddenly he realized the awful truth. He was supposed to be dead in that barn along with the others. His team had been hit and he was miraculously alive. He could not believe Joseph was a German agent.

If they planned to kill the entire team, less Joseph, then as soon as they checked the bodies they would know that he was still alive and they would start looking for him. Fear took over his mind and emotions as he instinctively started to run, but where to? As he ran, the limbs of the small bushes cut his face, and he had to keep his eyes partially closed to prevent them from being punctured. He did not know where he could go, but for the present he would keep running as far from the little barn as he could. He ran until he couldn't get his breath any longer. His mouth was dry and his heart was pounding so hard that he feared a heart attack. He fell on the ground trying to catch his breath. As he lay there panting, he still could not believe such a thing could happen. It was unthinkable for a team member to be a traitor.

After getting his breath and listening to make sure he was not followed, he began trying to think this disaster through. Joseph had to be a German spy. Someone had double-crossed them, and furthermore, it was never intended for them to assassinate Mussolini; it had to be a cover for something else - but what? As Tony lay on the ground trying to sort out the causes, before he realized it, he dropped off to asleep. Exhausted, he slept until dawn. Tony regained his composure after several hours of sleep.

Tony was a member of an OSS team on a mission; he would have to give a report of this tragic incident when he returned - if, in fact, he ever did. However, until he knew for sure what actually occurred, his report would not be accurate when he returned - if he ever did. Obviously it would be necessary to go back to see for himself if all the team had been killed, then try to make some sense out of what had happened.

After struggling up one hill and down another, he finally arrived to a point higher than where the little barn had been. As he visually surveyed the entire area, it appeared to be deserted. He pulled his berretta and slowly approached. At first glance he could not see any bodies for the burned rubble and ashes. Looking ahead as he stealthily crept along, he stumbled on something at his feet. When he looked down, the glassy eyes of Rick were staring up at him. As Tony looked around he saw the dead bodies of first one, then another, of his team members. Over-whelmed with grief, he could not control his weeping. He stood quietly in deep sorrow with tears streaming down his face wondering how could such a terrible thing happen to such a fine group of men. Realization eventually struck him, as he looked at the incredible destruction, that his best move would be to get out of there before he was discovered.

As he started to walk away from the scene of car-nage, he heard someone walking in his direction. He quickly ducked behind the partial remains of a wall. Hearing only one set of footsteps, he would have the drop on whoever it was. The man walked into the shattered barn and bent down to look at the bodies - it was Joseph. At first Tony wanted to shoot him and make him pay. However, reason persuaded him not to wipe out the only link he had to the horrible crime.

Joseph was shocked to see Tony standing before him with a pistol pointing straight at him. Joseph took a couple of small steps, as though to run, but he knew Tony would not miss.

Tony looked at Joseph as though he was a piece of garbage and said,
"Joseph, you have just one chance to stay alive, and that won't be for long if you don't cooperate and give me the answers I am looking for."

Joseph felt that Tony had absolutely no chance to get out of Italy alive, so why not tell him everything. He could buy some time and the next time they met Tony would be on the receiving end.

Joseph began, "I am a German agent. I was sent

to the United States to infiltrate the OSS and to be
sent back to Europe to learn about agents who were
working for the Allies. I did not choose this operation,
and I am sorry that I had to do what I did, but as a
good agent I do what I am told."

"You are a rat of the lowest order, Joseph. Did you
have anything to do with Colonel Mayhew's death?"

"Yes, I blew up the plane that was carrying Colonel
Mayhew. I was sorry about the others that had to die,
but they were in the wrong place at the wrong time.
Colonel Mayhew knew too much. He had stumbled
onto the real Alamo operation."

"The real Alamo operation - what do you mean?"

"The aim of the real Alamo operation was to assassinate the President, not Mussolini."

"The President!" exclaimed Tony.

"Yes, you see we were sent on a cover operation. We
have agents inside your OSS even in Washington,
DC. You have been working for one - you know him
as the Big Man."

Tony was in shock. "You mean Mantis is a German
spy?"

"Let's not call him a spy, let's just say he is a German
agent working for the good of Germany."

"When is this assassination attempt going to take
place?"

"In late November."

"I don't understand how you could be part of a government that seemingly has no sympathy for Jews -
even to the point of persecuting them."

"I am a victim, like so many others. My cooperation

with the German government is necessary if my father is to prosper, and my mother receive the necessary medical care she must have. It's a job to me and is purely based on getting paid for what I do."

"Are you telling me that you believe what you are doing is alright?" Tony asked in amazement.

"In your eyes Tony, it might not be, but the way I see things, it's just another job. Although unpleasant at times, it's still just a job. Not all Jews, have had it tough under the Nazis, some have become rich. You don't have one chance in a million of getting out of Italy alive. Your only salvation will for me to go to bat for you if you will agree to become a German agent."

Tony's face turned red as his blood pressure shot up suddenly, and gritting his teeth, he said firmly,

"You're crazy as a hoot owl Joseph. If that's what it takes to survive, then I won't make it. I am not going to be a dirty rotten German spy. I am not going to kill you Joseph, I'm not a cold-blooded killer like you are. I am going to tie you up and leave you to rot with your conscience. However, if I ever meet up with you again I will kill you - without hesitation."

"Tony, I am really sorry for your sake. I really hope you make it, but you won't. And, the same goes for you. To see you again is to kill you."

Tony tied Joseph's hands and feet tightly so he would be restrained indefinitely.

"Joseph, I would like to leave you something to remember me by." Tony remarked as he finished his task.

"What's that?" Asked Joseph.

"A bump on the head!" With that, Tony hit Joseph a blow on the head with his pistol that put him out like a light.

Now the mission of agent Tony De Angelo had drastically changed. He must warn the President of the United States of his impending assassination - but how?

The most urgent business at the present was to get away from this part of Italy. He had an uncle just outside of Naples, and if he could successfully make it there he would have a place to hide until he devised a plan.

Tony traveled by night and hid by day. By the second day he had decided that going to his uncle's house might not be the smart thing to do right away. His house could be staked out. To hide in a large city like Naples would be much easier. Menial jobs would be more readily available, and provide enough income to supply his immediate need of food and shelter.

Naples was a large city. It had a population of more than a million people. He could blend in and have no trouble mingling with the civilians, but the military might be an entirely different matter. All males of draft age had to carry some type of identification. He would have to find out what was required, then, by some means secure it through one of the residents. He had to avoid the Germans at all cost.

NAPLES ... a city to see, then die.

Tony did not want to think about dying, he had too

much to live for, and a very difficult mission to accomplish before he died. The problem immediately facing him was finding a job, and a place to live off the streets. He had limited work experience, but with very little effort he could become an expert busboy, waiter, or dishwasher. It was better to get a job in a café off the beaten path, one without a lot of military traffic; either Italian or German. The Italian civilian populace had suffered many restrictions, but when it came to eating, they made their opportunities. Italians continued to gather with family and friends and eat their favorite foods, and drink their favorite wine, regardless of a war. They were very inventive when it came to stretching the ingredients to make their favorite dishes.

Tony made his way into the Spacca-Napoli district of the city. It was the old part of town, and being a native Italian, he could blend in without any trouble. Getting a job at a small café as a clean up person should not be too difficult. The difficulty would be explaining his absence from the military.

Drifting through the section he stopped to inquire about a job in a couple of places only to be turned away. Finally he found a very small family owned and operated café in desperate need of someone with his particular skills. They were so happy to get him that they asked no questions. No one asked for proof of why he was not in the military, but sooner or later he would be questioned. The explanation used in the states would not work over here. He had to update the version to the current situation. He was wounded in Ethiopia, shot in the back, and spent months in the hospital in Rome. He was discharged because of his injury, which prohibited him from serving in the military. As he explained his situation about needing a room, a couple of the men working there generously offered to share their room with him.

Tony worked ten hours a day. He began settling in and in actuality he was feeling safe and felt free to talk to the local people. He was the youngest of the men working at the café. Boys too young hung around the doors trying to pick up extra jobs. Because of his age the shortage of men in Naples created strong competition among the signorinas. Tony was not interested in any of them, but he did have to be sociable and not appear to be unfriendly. He began to think about Betty now that he had some leisure time. The majority of the Italian girls had coal black hair, and either brown or black eyes, quite the opposite of Betty. He wondered if his longing to see her would ever become a reality. By now she could be married, and since she didn't know what had become of him, had given him up for dead, or simply didn't care about him anymore.

One evening one of the women had a visit from an Italian officer. Tony wasn't aware that the officer was in the café until he entered the dining room to clean off a table. The signorina waved to Tony, which attracted the officer's attention. Now Tony was in the spotlight. He ducked his head and moved to the kitchen in great haste. The officer gave Tony a long hard once over, making him very uncomfortable.

'Well,' he thought, 'maybe he'll forget all about the incident.'

After the officer left, one of the waiters came to Tony.

"I heard that officer was asking Maria why you were not in the army. She told him you had been, but you were out because of your wound."

'Maybe that will be the end of it,' thought Tony.

The next day the same Italian officer came to see Maria and brought a German officer with him. They asked that Tony wait on their table. The manager explained that that was highly irregular, but if they insisted, Tony could serve their table.

Tony was in shock. He just knew that the German was up to something and maybe had identified him. Tony limped very noticeably as he walked from their table to the kitchen. The German officer could speak Italian, however he chose to just watched intensely. Tony had a spooked feeling - he knew this was not good. Finally the meal was served, the two officers ate their dinner, and left the café. He could not be in the café the next day. They could have him arrested and checked out.

Tony did his usual clean up after the café closed. He had hidden his knapsack under the counter earlier, and when most everyone had left the kitchen he slipped some bread, cheese, and a bottle of wine into it and quietly left the café and headed out of town as fast as he could. He had no choice now but to go to his uncle's farm.

The farm was just outside the little town of

Anderetta, southeast of Naples. After two days of walking and hiding, Tony arrived at his uncle's farm. Papa De Angelo was very happy to see his nephew. He had not seen Tony since he was a young teenage boy back in Cisterna. Papa had made a little money working on the projects around Anzio, then went south and made a down payment on this little farm.

Tony tried to bring Papa up to date on the family back in America. He did not know how to explain to him about his job with the OSS. He just simply stated that it was a job for the U.S. Government.

The activities on the farm had become routine. He had never wanted to be a farmer caring for livestock, and pruning grape vines, but at the present it wasn't a bad life. The farm was quite a way from the little town, therefore any strangers would be noticed at once. He had informed his uncle that he was hiding, and asked him not to give out any information about him, but he didn't tell him the reason.

Since the Allies had invaded Sicily on July 10, 1943 the attitude of the Italian people had greatly changed. They now feared an invasion by the Allies. The bombing of Rome on July 19th had caused terror among the civilians who witnessed the air attack. There were mixed emotions about fighting the Americans and British.

The partisans were growing in numbers each day while waiting for the right time to overthrow the Fascist. They wanted freedom from the Germans as well, and a democratic government for Italy. The majority of the Italian people still believed that Italy would not be defeated in this war. They had been kept in the dark about losses in Africa and the certainty of their defeat with the Germans in Sicily. As ancient history reveals - if Sicily falls so will Italy.

Sicily did fall on August 17, 1943, and so did the hopes of the Fascist. Mussolini was kicked out of office, leaving the Fascist without a leader. The Italian people had to appear supportive of their government even though they did not agree. They were in a difficult spot. They wanted the Allies to win, but how could they not support their own government.

Just when Tony began to feel secure at his uncle's farm they had a visitor. Tony was out in the vineyard working when the man talked to his uncle. The visitor questioned his uncle's loyalty, which was quickly declared. He wanted to know if he had a young man working for him on his farm. Uncle De Angelo remembered Tony's instructions - "do not reveal my presence." Looking the man straight in the eyes, he answered,

"There was a man helping me on the farm, but he has gone. He moved away a couple of days ago, and I don't know where he went."

Tony had slipped around to the back of the little barn so he could hear the conversation.

"Did this man come from Naples?"

"I do not know where he came from," was the uncle's reply.

After hearing the question about Naples, Tony had a gut feeling that this man was on his trail - but why?

Tony quickly made up his mind to get away from

there. He and his uncle decided that he should hide out in the hills and return after midnight for food. There would be a lamp in the window if it were safe to return. This schedule was maintained for several days, until there was another visit from a different stranger looking for a young man on the farm.

In the meantime the British had invaded the toe of the Italian peninsula. At first the Italians assumed it was the Americans. Tony thought this was his means of escape, but since it turned out to be the British he discarded the idea.

Tony had just returned from his Uncle's house to his hide out to take a nap, when he heard distant rumblings and saw flashes in the sky to the west near the coast. For almost an hour this activity continued. He had never seen flashes or heard noise before - what could it mean?

About mid-morning the road below him became clogged with heavy traffic going toward the west in the direction of the noise. By mid-afternoon the road was filled with civilians going in the opposite direction of the vehicles. He had to find out what was going on. It was risky, but these people were worried about themselves, not about a deserter.

He approached a group of women resting by the roadside.
"What's going on?"
"The Americans are coming."
"How do you know?"
"The soldiers told us. They are down on the coast and are coming this way."

"Are you sure?"

The women did not answer, but picked up their bags and headed up the road. Tony's pulse raced as he thought this was a way out of Italy - well, hopefully. If he could get up with the Americans, maybe they would believe him. It was almost dark and time to move.

He waited until after midnight before returning to the farm. He and his uncle talked until almost dawn. Tony told his uncle that he had a very important mission to carry out and must get back to America.

"A very important official in the government in America is in danger of being killed. I must go and try to save him."

"But how Tony?"

"I don't know Papa, but I have no choice but to try, and by all that's in me, I must succeed."

Papa packed Tony's knapsack with cheese, bread, and two bottles of wine.

"Papa, I know you don't understand, but maybe someday you will."

They put their arms around each other and kissed as Tony pushed away.

"Grazie, Papa; arrivederci."

Tony put his knapsack over his shoulder, and slowly walked down the hill as he looked back to see Papa waving and calling in a loud voice - "arrivederci, Tony."

In the distance he could see Papa wiping tears from his cheeks. This was truly a bittersweet moment.

TWENTY-FOUR

T he body of Luis had been found and identified. He had been shot three times in the back and his throat cut. The local police determined that he had been robbed, and because of his resistance had been killed. There was little the OSS or the FBI could do. With the information supplied by Jo and the method of Luis's death, it was very clear that for some reason they had suspected him. If it could be determined what had caused the gang to suspect Luis, at least it would be a clue as to the future of Jo and Rafael. Rafael contacted Charley Wells, who in turn passed the information along to the FBI and the OSS.

The death of Agent MacLaughlin was a blow to the FBI, and cause for alarm for the OSS. Charles Wells drove his jeep to a prearranged meeting place. There were two FBI agents just in from Washington, DC to meet with him.

"What do you think Charley - do we have a leak?"

"It looks like it. We just can't figure how they got wise to Mac. Of course the locals are saying it was a robbery, but we know better."

"How is the girl singer doing?"

"Well, if you are asking about her singing, it's going over in a big way. She has fingered a couple of the late night visitors to be outsiders, probably Germans or locals who speak German. Jo has over- heard some conversations that make it convincing that out-siders visit the club late at night."

"What about a plan to get her out in case of real dan-ger. You know there are a lot of people in high places following this case because of her."

"Yes, I know. We have a plan that we feel can be exe-cuted to get her out of harms way. "

"Charley, do you think we should try and get anoth-er agent into the club to replace Mac?"

"No, there is too much risk in doing that. I doubt that they would be willing to hire another waiter just now. You know if they did they would leave no stone unturned to find out all they could about the new man. Additionally, we just don't have another agent suitable for the job."

"You know Charley, we were not aware of Mac's death when we left Washington. We were ordered down here from the top to bring them up to date on the progress of this investigation. You know there is real concern about an operation that could in some way damage the canal."

"There is one side that feels the canal could be properly defended with our anti-aircraft guns. Another side is concerned that such tactics, used on occasions by the Japanese called "Kamikaze" meth-ods, could penetrate our air defenses no matter how many guns we have. Washington is convinced that something big is in the mill, and we will continue to believe the threat will be coming from the northern coast of Columbia."

"Couldn't the Army Air Force send recon planes along the coast to spot any possible landing strips?"

"Yes Charley, but if they are off the coast some distance cutting a landing strip and assembling planes, it would be difficult to pinpoint a well camouflaged area, and for that reason it would be easy to conclude that there were no landing strips, or planes being assembled. We are going to have to get a more specific location before we can begin to take pictures."

"We have got to move on this mission and get some confirmation, or the brass back in Washington will take another route to find out what is going on."

"Okay, I will get word to Rafael and Jo that we must start pressing for information; even to the point of taking chances of tipping our hand."

"Alright Charley, let's get to it! You know there has been increased German U-boat activity in this part of the Gulf in recent weeks. Could be that they are bringing in parts of planes, or other means of damaging the canal."

"What other means? Charley asked.

"Well, I know this might sound far fetched, but it has been confirmed that the Germans are experimenting with rockets. We don't know how successful they have been, but suppose they could successfully use rockets against the canal. There is real concern in Washington about such a capability; we have no defensive against these weapons. They could be launched from smaller areas than landing strips, and would be much easier to conceal. It is felt by Army Intelligence that the most logical place for such an attack would be the Gatun Locks. Keep in touch, Charley."

Jo was on the inside now, and had established herself as a singer that drew the crowds, which made money for the club. It would be unwise to try and pull she and Rafael out of the investigation. They understood the risks, and that was the name of the game. Besides, Carlos had taken the bait - he had made it known he was pursuing Jo for his personal girlfriend.

Jo went shopping early the next day, and as planned, met with Charley Wells the civilian. Charley seemed depressed and very nervous.

"Jo, the pressure is on from Washington. We are going to have to come up with something concrete or this operation will be scrapped. Our careers with our respective organizations will be finished."

"What can I do that I am not already doing, Charley?"

"You are going to have to get more information from Carlos. He is the key and you might have to take chances, but that is the course we will have to take."

"How," asked Jo.

"Find out about the men that come into the club late at night. You might casually chat with one of them and try and pull some information. We have got to know what, if anything, is going on and where it is happening."

"Charley I just don't think Carlos is going to tell me anything of any consequence. All he wants me to do is become his girlfriend, and even then I don't think he will talk. You know he offered me half of the income from the shows if I would move in with him."

"You don't have to do that Jo, under any circumstances."

"You know Charley, your suggestion about getting one of the workmen to talk might work if he were drunk."

"You got any ideas, Jo?"

Jo stopped by one of the shops, purchased a red and black scarf and a straw hat just to justify her absence from the club and prove she did go shopping.

A couple of nights later three men came into the club that Jo had seen in there previously. She heard one of them say, "It's good to get out of the jungle and back to civilization."

This man spoke English. What would an American be doing here at the club?

Jo let fifteen or so minutes pass, then casually sauntered over to their table, and looking down at the American, asked,

"Want to buy me a drink, handsome?"

He looked shocked. "You mean me?"

"Sure."

It was the perfect time for Jo to try her luck, since Carlos was out of the club on some kind of business.

"You know I got plenty of money to have a . . .

"What are you saying?" Asked Jo. Realizing that her companion was becoming incoherent.

"You know what I mean - a party every night."

"Tell me," urged Jo, "what do you do to make so

much money?"

"Shh, don't tell anyone but I drive one of them dirt pushers." He slurred.

"Oh, you mean a bulldozer."

"Yeah, but don't tell anyone, it's a secret."

"Do you work around town?"

"Are you kidin? I work in the jungle."

Jo did not want to push this man too hard, but he seemed willing to talk as he put his arm around Jo's neck - which she did not discourage.

"Oh, are you building a road?"

"You know that's the dumbest thing about what I'm doing, it looks like a road, but it don't go nowhere."

"You mean it's not completed yet?"

"Naw, I am telling you it is almost done and it don't go no where. They're through with me and I don't have to go back anymore. All they're doing now is rolling. That's why you and I are going to have a big time baby. I'm going to be around for a long time to make you happy."

He tried to pull Jo over closer to him and kiss her, but she gently pushed him away.

"Not here. Wait until we're alone."

In an effort to get more specific information, she let him hold her hand.

"I have heard that there's some construction work going on in Columbia. Did you work there?"

"Shhh-h-h - - - yeah I did some work there, but don't you tell anybody; they told me not to tell a soul. But, since you're going to be my girlfriend, I can trust you, can't I"?

"Honey, you know you can."

Jo keep pumping him. "The road that I heard they were building in Columbia was along the coast."

"It might be, but the road, or whatever I worked on, was a good five miles from the gulf and only about ten miles inside Columbia, can you beat that."

At least Jo got a rough idea of where the strip might be.

"You know there were some funny talking people that came to the work site the other day. I never heard people talk like they did."

Jo thought. 'Could be German or Japanese.'

There was no doubt in Jo's mind that this man had been working on an airstrip in Columbia that could be used for the possible bombing of the canal. Jo felt that she had the information she had been after, now to get it to the proper authorities.

Unknown to Jo, Carlos had returned to the club and had been observing her conversation with a man she should not be talking to. He asked one of the waiters if he knew what the conversation was about.

"All I heard was the man telling about his work with a dirt machine. Then Jo asked him if it was a bull-dozer."

Carlos viewed the conversation as out of order, and promptly became very suspicious.

He turned to a waiter. "Go tell Jo that it's time for her to sing, and if she doesn't have a number ready make one up."

Carlos turned to one of the bouncers.

"Get that drunk and bring him to my office."

Rafael was close enough to hear the orders of Carlos and he knew now that the trap was about to be sprung. Jo was in serious trouble.

A prearranged signal was for him to hang a tablecloth on the little tree that stood outside the back entrance. Rafael didn't see anyone as he stepped out, so he spread the tablecloth over the little tree; he just prayed that Charley or some other agent was on the job. When the lookout saw the tablecloth he was to immediately notify the base; who would in turn send MPs to the club to rescue Jo. Unknown to Rafael, the FBI and the OSS had decided to pull him out at the same time. They feared that Carlos might be onto him too, and after Jo's departure there would be no need to expose him to the dangers of being identified.

Carlos had a reception committee, consisting of three killers, waiting for the customer who visited with Jo. As he was hustled toward the back office he shouted with a loud voice.

"What's the trouble? You can't take me away from my girlfriend!"

He had been literally dragged into the office where he was hit across the mouth, causing a stream of blood to run down his chin. The blow made him stagger and seemingly half conscious. After a bucket of cold water was dumped on his head, he regained his equilibrium and he tried to push up from the chair. About that time one of the men grabbed him by the hair of his head, and looked him square in the eyes from a distance of six inches.

"You have just one chance of remaining healthy for

the rest of your life - now tell us about your conversation with the young lady."

"I don't think that is any of your business."

"I don't believe you completely understand. If I slit your throat from ear to ear you will then understand that we mean business." With a flick of the wrist he slit a small gash in the man's throat.

"The next time, I will go about three inches deeper. Do you understand?"

"Please, please, don't hurt me. I was only talkin' to the girl about the work I been doing in the jungle."

"What kind of work have you been doing that would be of interest to our singer?"

"I told her that I had been running a dirt moving machine building a short road in the jungle. She wanted to know where this short road was? I told her it was in Columbia."

Carlos stood back from the huddle; his eyes flashing fire and his face flushed.

"Get him out of here!"

Under his breath he said to the last man out of his office, "Get rid of him for good."

Carlos made a phone call, then, sat down in his chair holding his head.

Some time later there was a knock at the door.

"Come in!" shouted Carlos.

A man, dressed somewhat differently than most men around Panama, entered the room.

"Herr Schiller we have a problem." Carlos declared.

"One that cannot be solved?" He asked glibly.

Carlos laid out what he had obtained from the unfortunate dozer driver.

"I don't believe the driver talked to anyone else. We have taken care of him permanently. As for the girl, that is another matter. She will not be allowed to leave the club."

Carlos felt betrayed by Jo. His feelings had not changed toward her; his crush on her was still there, and he did not want to lose her.

"How do you know she will not talk to someone in the club that could be an agent?"

"I know my people, and none are connected to any intelligence organization in sympathy with the United States."

"You really don't know that, do you Carlos? Herr Schiller asked in a sarcastic voice.

"Make sure someone you trust stays with her until the club is closed, then we must get rid of her. There is too much at stake to have one person destroy all we have accomplished. We are too near the completion of our mission. Get rid of her - tonight!"

Carlos was deeply pained at the thought, yet he knew the orders of Herr Schiller had to be carried out.

Herr Schiller had almost closed the door when he turned slowly and walked back into the office.

"On second thought Carlos, let's get your singer into your office and see if she really is a singer or perhaps something else - you know, like a spy. Let's make sure all of your employees are as faithful and pure as you say."

Herr Schiller again reached the door to exit the office when he turned and looked at Carlos with cold steely

eyes. "Make sure there is no slip up, do you understand?"

Carlos could only think of one thing - they will torture her to make her talk. If she is an American agent
it will look bad for me, since I have been giving her
cover. Carlos was a man with no feelings when it
came to making money and dealing with the kind of
people he had around him - but Jo was something
different, she was special, and he could not put his
feelings for her out of his mind.

He knew she could not stand the torture they
would put her through. They would destroy her beautiful face, and lovely body, then, in the end kill her.
Carlos was torn between two choices. To let them tear
her to pieces, or kill her before the club closed. He
cared for her too much to do either. He would get
someone else to do the job, but that would not
remove the responsibility - he would be the guilty
one.

It would have to be someone other than those he
normally used. They might themselves rape and torture her before killing her. It must be a professional
job - no warning - no pain. Rafael had such a reputation when he came into the club. Carlos had a feeling when he hired Rafael that he was hiding from
something in his past - maybe it was murder?"

Carlos walked out of his office and caught the eye
of Rafael and motioned him into the office. Carlos
didn't beat around the bush.
"Rafael I have a job for you. I want it done before the
club closes."

"What kind of a job?"

"I want you to get rid of someone for me. No pain - with a knife. Can you do it for me?"

After the sudden shock, Rafael's mind began to spin. What is this? Have they found out about me and want me to become a partner in crime to prove myself. I have to play along, but I can't murder any-one; maybe I can fake it.

"Who is this person", asked Rafael.

"Jo, and I want a clean job."

Rafael almost lost his breath - his stomach rolled so loud that the he feared Carlos would hear it. He had to hold one hand with the other to keep the shaking from being noticed. To remain cool at this stage was a must. To show any emotion might give Carlos cause for concern for him also.

"Here is a knife. I want you to take her into her dress-ing room after she finishes her set. I will make it worth your while."

"Why Jo? She is such a nice kid and a money maker for your club."

"We have reason to believe she is an American spy."

Sweat began popping out onto Rafael's brow. Jo was in desperate need of rescue - maybe he was too. Could it be that they wanted him to kill Jo, and then get rid of him?

Rafael picked up the knife, folded it and put it in his pocket. The blade was five inches long. Just long enough to pierce a heart with one plunge. The natives preferred to slit the throat.

Rafael had no choice but to play along with

Carlos. He went out back of the club and placed another white cloth in the small tree for the warning that they needed help immediately. Maybe they would see two of them. He knew if the MPs didn't get to them in time it would all be over for both of them.

It was now time for Jo's last performance of the night. She usually sang three songs and then let the audience select a couple of their favorites before leaving the stage. Somehow Rafael had to get some kind of warning to her. He quickly wrote on a small piece of paper sing ... sing ... sing. Jo had on a blouse that was low cut in the front. As Rafael walked by her with a tray in his hand he dropped the note down her front knowing she would feel it, and he hoped she would read it. She never moved or made an attempt to get the note. Rafael was afraid he had missed, and the note had fallen harmlessly onto the floor. He watched as Jo went into the ladies room. He wondered if she understood the note. It was the only way they could remain alive - stall for the MPs. Stall meant singing until they did arrive.

The audience was Latin; there were no GIs at the club since it was after curfew. Now that she had read the note it was up to her. Jo started her show with the most liked tunes. As she sang she tried desperately to read Rafael's mind and try to understand what he meant by sing ... sing ... sing. Was it some kind of a code she was suppose to know, but didn't. Her performance went off without a hitch, three songs, then requests. After singing her usual three request songs, she started to leave the stage, when

Rafael became a one man cheering section. He came to the front and started applauding and yelling for more. Jo knew this was most unusual, but since Rafael liked her singing she would at least sing just one more for him. Rafael was in a cold sweat and was all but crying aloud for the MPs to come to their rescue. As Jo finished her number, Rafael again called for one more. His actions had attracted the attention of the bouncers. They thought he might have been drinking and didn't interfere. After four encore numbers, Jo waved to the crowd, "mucho gracias."

She went into her dressing room where she found Rafael with a knife in his hand. "Wha -a -a - t?" Rafael quickly put his hand over her mouth, so she couldn't make a sound, while he told her the situation.

"Jo the only chance we have is to hold up in here and hope the MPs make it in time. I can stall for a short time because they think I'm killing you, which should take a few minutes; but our time is very limited.

They had been in the room alone but for five minutes or so when there was a knock at the door - it was Carlos.

"Rafael, are you about through?"

"Yeah, just a little clean up." Before he could finish Carlos interrupted.

"I don't want to hear the details."

Rafael and Jo could only stay in the small dressing room until the door was knocked down. There was no other way out.

There was a sudden louder knock at the door.

"We have orders to pick up a package from this room;

open the door!"

"I can't right now I am busy," was Rafael's reply.

"Busy doing what?"

Rafael did not answer.

They went away but not for long. They returned with a fire ax and started chopping the door. Jo grabbed Rafael tightly, and they clung to one another just waiting for the end.

Above the banging on the door, they could also hear a lot of commotion from inside the club. They heard the unmistakable firing of shots; then the entire club turned into a shooting gallery. Rafael made Jo lay down on the floor in case someone decided to spray the dressing room.

"Could it be the MPs," whispered Jo.

Rafael did not answer, but he was thinking to himself - how could two MPs rescue them from all those armed people in the club. The shooting went on for another five or so minutes; then it stopped.

It was easy to believe that the MPs had lost. Now they would have to face the truth - their time had run out.

They heard noise outside the dressing room door that sounded like chairs being drug across the floor. Then to their surprise and relief they heard their names called out as they recognized the voice of Charley Wells."Jo, Jo, are you in there?"

"Oh, yes, Charley, we are in here."

"Come on out, the war is over."

The club was in shambles. Carlos was dead, so was Herr Schiller and most of the employees of the club.

TWENTY - FIVE

Two days after her rescue at the club, Jo, now Betty Peterson, was on a plane headed for the good old U.S.A. along with Charley and David.

The FBI and OSS had sorted out what happened in Panama, for the most part. They felt that although there was still a slight possibility of some act of sabotage against the canal, the major threat had been abolished. The ring was broken, the German influence was identified, and eliminated; therefore it would be safe to speculate that no foreign espionage organization could be established again. The defense against German subs in the immediate area was getting stronger each day and Germany would have to turn more of their attention to the defense of their homeland. Our reconnaissance of the area would now be more diligent and efficient.

Betty had heard bits and pieces of what happened at the club that fateful night. Now that she had the undivided attention of Charley, she would attempt to learn all the details. The FBI talks very little about good stuff.

"Charley, I want to know what happened while David and I were barricaded in my dressing room?"

"Betty, you would be much better off not to know."

"Oh come on Charley, tell me."

"You did not know it, but the original plan for getting you out of the club was for the MPs to come into the club to arrest you for being AWOL. We knew you were in trouble, but the timing was off since your crisis occurred after hours. You can thank the FBI for thinking ahead and having the Panamanian Police accompany the MPs."

"Charley, please thank the FBI for me."

"I will. When the MPs attempted to gain entrance to the club they were refused. The club was within legal rights and could have held out, but when the police arrived with a search warrant and twenty men, they had to go into a defensive mode. They slammed the door, but the police broke it down with axes, and that was when the shooting started. The police lost three men and several more were wounded. As you know Carlos and most of his henchmen were put out of action. The club will be closed for the duration."

"That was some battle you boys went through just to rescue me."

"Wait a minute Betty, they came for me too," added David.

They all laughed briefly, but it didn't last as they thought about the close call they both had, and the cost of the operation.

After the briefing, there was mutual silence as each reflected on their inner thoughts. After some time, the plane dropped from the sky to land in Miami. Once they enjoyed two days of eating, and sleeping, they were required to take complete physicals. One of the problems with serving in the Panama Canal area was exposure to malaria. They hoped they had not been infected, but it would be some time before they would know for sure.

Betty took a short shopping trip to purchase some new civilian clothes. The army duds had to go.

The plane was loaded and taxied down to the runway. After a short wait the engines were throttled up and they were off for home - Washington DC. T/5 Mary McCullum, Jo Dutton, was now Betty Peterson. At least for now she could be herself. She had done her service, which turned out to be more than she bargained for. Yet it was a good feeling to know one had done a service for her country to help bring victory in this war.

After much needed sleep, there was time to get excited about returning to civilization. Hot baths, good food, and some chocolate candy - even though made with substitute sugar - would still be good. Washington renewed memories of the one she was afraid to think of. Tony. Was he still alive? Does he still love me as I love him? Maybe someday she would know. The war could not last forever. There was one thing she would not do on her return, and that was ask for an assignment out of the country.

As they walked up the ramp to the terminal, an FBI agent met them. He drove them to their respective organizations: David to the FBI, and Betty to the

OSS.

Betty went to the office of her section chief and identified herself to the secretary, thinking there would be the usual wait. Before she could sit down the door opened and the chief bounded out wearing a big smile.

"Betty, let me say on behalf of the OSS, and myself, we are extremely proud of you and the work you did. You took a giant step for the advancement of women agents in the FBI. They will no doubt have a different attitude toward female agents now. You will, of course, be personally congratulated by the proper people in the Bureau."

"Thank you chief, you don't know how much I appreciate your kind words. I wanted so much to do a good job for the agency."

"Well, you did!"

"Betty, you will meet with Charley and David tomorrow with the top brass from the OSS and Army Intelligence for a final debriefing."

"Chief, we need a current worldwide briefing on the war situation. We have heard nothing since we have been out of touch and I am very interested in the war in Europe."

"I promise that you three will have a special up to the minute progress of the war."

"What about the war in Europe, Chief?"

"Right now the Americans and British are cleaning up Sicily. After the debriefing session is over, be sure to come back to my office Betty."

"Sure chief, I will."

As promised, Betty returned to the chief's office after the big debriefing with the brass.

"Well Betty, how did the meeting go?"

"Fine chief, I was embarrassed by the things that were said about me. Such words were more than I deserved."

"Don't feel that way; you did a good job and those weird people that sent you on such a risky mission thought you deserved every word of praise, and then some."

"Now that this mission is over; what's next chief?"

"Well Betty, you are going to get a two week leave and you can spend it anywhere you please."

Betty thought - 'a two week leave. Where can I go and what can I do? If only Tony were here to spend it with me. I can go back to Memphis and see the folks, or maybe stay in Washington and attend some of the parties.' None of that was very appealing. She had no one she could buddy with in Washington or in Memphis either. Memphis would bring back such sad memories of Tony, Carl, and a myriad of others things, and Washington was full of wolves seeking whom they might devour. Until she got over Tony, or married that boy, she just couldn't get interested in any other man.

"Hey, where did you go Betty? I thought you would be excited about a two week leave."

"Sorry chief, I guess I let my thoughts take over and I forgot where I was for the moment."

"You can start your leave today - right now in fact."

"Thanks, I will."

Betty had gotten to the elevator when the thought suddenly hit her. If the OSS and the FBI are so impressed with her services, why shouldn't she ask them for a favor - particularly the OSS.

With an about face she headed for the chief's office. The secretary was on the phone, so she had to wait for a few moments.

"Yes, may I help you?"

"Would you see if the chief can see me for a few more minutes?"

"Sure, just a minute while I check."

"Betty, the chief said to come right in."

"Well, Betty I bet you forgot to tell me something."

"As a matter of fact chief I did. Not to tell you something but to ask a favor of you."

"Consider it done, Betty. What is this big favor?"

"You know I have a special friend that is a member of the OSS and was assigned to a team called Alamo and sent to Europe. I have not heard from him since he left the states. I don't know if he is still overseas, in the states, or even alive. I would consider it a great personal favor if you could find out about my friend. His name is Tony De Angelo."

"Obviously this man is much more than just a friend; but you know what you are asking is impossible. You know as well as I do that information about an active operation is top secret."

"I understand chief, but I feel the OSS owes me one and I am calling in a favor."

"You must know that I know nothing about such an operation, nor that such an operation ever existed, but because of you I will make every effort to locate your friend and his current status."

"Will you? I will always be grateful."

" You will have to give me time."

"I understand chief, and I will try and be patient."

"Where can you be reached in Washington?"

"I will let your secretary know my location as soon as I find a place, which won't be easy."

"You're right about that. Unless you can move in with some girlfriend, getting on a waiting list is about all you can do. I know it won't be like having your own apartment, but you know we have some rooms that are used by our people who come in from out of town. Why don't you stay in one of them until you can find something better?"

"That's extremely kind of you chief - I will take you up on your offer."

Betty had stayed in her room at the agency for a couple of days hoping for a telephone call about Tony, but none came. She had tried to get in touch with Larry Roberts, but was told he was out of town. Being alone for the first time in months was getting to her. She would appreciate seeing anyone from the past. What else can a single girl do in a big city, but go shopping. While on a shopping trip she had a stroke of good luck. She was walking toward the entrance of a department store when she heard her name called.

"Betty! Betty! Where have you been?"

The door of the cab flew open and out jumped Roger. He was now a Major, but that increase in rank had not changed his good looks - her heart quickened.

"Betty it's so good to see you."

"Well Roger, I can surely say the same."

"Have you been in Washington all this time and I did-n't know it?"

"No, I have been out of the country on an assign-ment."

"Well, let's forget the past and start anew. Come go to lunch with me."

"Sure, I am hungry."

The lunch was pleasant for both of them. Just having someone to talk with was a treat for Betty.

"Roger I owe you an apology for the way I acted on our last date."

"You mean the Mayflower thing?"

"Yes, I am truly sorry."

"Forget it Betty. You can prove how really sorry you are by going with me back to the Mayflower tonight."

"I would really like to Roger, but do you think we can get reservations this late?"

"Leave it up to ole Roger. I'll pick you up at eight - okay?'

"That will be great. Is Harry James playing there?"

"I don't know, but it will be someone good. We can push and shove with everyone else on the dance floor."

Roger was lucky enough to get a table, even though it was about three rows from the dance floor. The music was good, and as expected, the dance floor was crammed full of bodies clinging to one another making an effort to dance.

After dinner, and several dances, Roger began to

talk about their future. He wanted to see Betty the next day, and the next and the next. Betty didn't want to admit it, but she was really enjoying Roger's company.

Around 2:00 a.m., when they made their way to Betty's door, she immediately saw a note hanging on the doorknob. Thinking it might be urgent; she opened the note and read it aloud.

'Betty you should call me as soon as you return.' Signed - Chief.

Betty had another one of those cold chills run through her body - what now? Could this be another assignment?

"Roger, you will have to go, I want to call the chief."

"You don't mean you are going to get him out of bed at this hour?"

"He said as soon as possible. I had a wonderful time, now kiss me good night Roger."

Roger reached to embrace Betty with both arms.

"No Roger, just a kiss, not an embrace."

Betty closed the door, took a deep breath and dialed the chief's number; then it hit her. This was not about another assignment - it was about Tony! A sleepy voice on the other end,

"Hello."

"Chief, this is Betty."

"Betty are you at your place?"

"Yes sir."

"Don't go to bed, I will be right over."

"What is this all about, Chief?"

"I will fill you in just a few minutes."

The phone went dead and now all she could do was sit, and try to guess what was coming.

Two fifteen in the morning seemed like a good time to put on a pot of coffee. A half hour later, there was a knock on the door. Betty opened the door to see Mr. Peterson and the Chief.

"Oh, what a surprise. It's so good to see you Mr. Peterson."

"Betty, how are you?"

"Fine."

"You know I was out of town when you got back, or I would have been in on the welcoming committee."

"Stop kidding, I don't believe it!"

Both laughed and then hugged.

"I have made some fresh coffee, would you'all like a cup?"

"Sure", they both said in unison.

"I have some cookies too; although they are not very sweet - wartime you know."

"I don't want any cookies," replied Mr. Peterson, "but if you have some cheese and crackers, I will take you up on that."

"Sure, I am from the south and you know cheese and crackers are a standard item for a southern kitchen."

Betty went to her little fridge, all the time trying to guess what these two important men came to see her about at this unearthly hour. The suspense was killing her, yet she was afraid to ask. Betty offered them more coffee.

"May I refill your cup Mr. Peterson?"

"No, I have plenty Betty, thank you."

"Betty we want you to know how much we appreciate your dedication and service to the OSS. You have in many ways set the standards that will be used for years to come. We are here this morning because of our feelings for you. We would do anything in our power to make life smooth for you. But we know also that you are a good soldier."

"What are you trying to say Mr. Peterson?"

"Betty it is our sorrowful duty to give you some bad news."

Betty gasped and bit her lip; for she now knew this meeting was about Tony.

"Betty we have thoroughly investigated this case and I feel our assessment of the situation is very accurate."

"What is it chief?" asked Betty in a weak voice.

"The mission that Tony was assigned to called Alamo has met with foul play. The team was hit. By whom we don't know, but by all indications it was complete. They were operating just south of Rome. Their mission was to take out the dictator of Italy. We have tried to piece together what actually happened, but so far have failed. We contacted the British MI-6 for help and they sent a man into the area, but could find nothing. The only confirmation that can be considered reliable comes from the partisans. We know the team had been working in the area, because we had radio contact with them from to time to time. But as of this date the team, nor any of its members, can be located. It is believed that they are all dead or probably worse; prisoners of the Gestapo."

Betty had been in shock during the entire time of the chief's report.

"Is there hope? Any hope at all?" she asked.

There was no response.

"I can't believe that Tony is dead."

"Let's don't give up completely Betty. We have other agents in Italy and maybe Tony, or others of the team, will show up with them. We will continue to investigate this operation with both the OSS and the FBI."

Betty had to ask one more time.

"What are the chances of finding Tony alive?"

"You know Betty until we receive confirmed details that all the members of the team are dead or captured, there is always reason to believe that they are alive. There is always a fifty-fifty chance."

Betty closed the door after her visitors left. It also felt as though she had just closed the door to the remainder of her life. Sometime later the morning began to dawn, ushering in a new day. She had not moved from her chair all night. What's the use, she thought. There is no beginning now - just the end.

For two days she stayed in her apartment. The blinds were closed, and the phone was off the hook. She had hardly eaten any food, nor taken a shower. As she walked by a small mirror hanging on the wall, she saw herself for the first time since she received the news about Tony. She could hardly believe that it was her reflection in the mirror. Tony would not be proud of her. He had always complemented the way she looked. Now she had even lost her self-respect.

'I am not giving up. Tony is not dead.' She determined.

She walked over to the phone, put it back on the hook, opened the blinds and headed for the bathroom to wash her hair and take a much needed shower. Before she could get into the shower the phone rang. "Hello!"

"Betty I have been trying to reach you since yesterday. Are your alright; your phone has been out of order."

"I am alright Mr. Peterson. My phone has been off the hook."

"Betty how about dinner with me tonight? You need to get out; I will not take no for an answer."

"You don't have to do that Mr. Peterson, but I do feel hungry and will take you up on food."

"Fine, I will pick you up at seven."

The dinner was excellent as well as sumptuous. Mr. Peterson was going out of his way to cheer her up. Betty wondered why he was doing this. Was he interested in her personally?

"Mr. Peterson, are you married with three kids?"

"No, I am not married at the present, and I do not have any children; but if you are interested I might be persuaded to reverse my marital status."

"That was a very nice compliment, but I just wondered if you had someone to tell your troubles to."

"No, I don't. I keep pretty busy and at the present I really don't miss being married, but when the war is over I plan to settle down, and if you are available I would like to give some young buck a run for his money."

"Mr. Peterson, you cause me to blush."

"Seriously Betty, how would you like to spend some time out at the farm? We have a new class of recruits and your experience would be invaluable. We have a couple of women members of the class and they would be especially interested in what you might have to say. I know you are still on leave, but if you are willing we really need you."

I know he's just trying to be nice to me, but why not? She asked herself.

"Okay Mr. Peterson, I will be glad to."

"Fine, a car will pick you up in the morning at seven.

As the car slowly moved through the gate, she realized she was looking for Tony and not at the grounds. She noticed that quite a few changes had been made at the farm. There were a lot more people now and security was much tighter than when she was there previously.

Betty was assigned to a room and given a schedule. Her instruction class would be each morning from 09:30 til 11:00 hours. She could talk about anything she cared to, but of course they wanted her to relate to her experiences from her last mission.

Things had settled into routine, and Betty was recognized as a veteran instructor. She was enjoying her class because it kept her thoughts from reverting back to the past.

On Friday morning, when the class was in full swing, Betty was telling the students about her singing. The class got a big laugh as Betty described the band. Then there was a knock on the classroom door, followed by one of the instructors entering the room. He handed Betty a note that simply said, 'Report to the office.'

Puzzled, "Am I to leave now?"

"Yes, I will take over for you. Go to the supervisor's office at the main building."

'What in the world have I done now?' Betty mumbled to herself. 'Don't tell me that I am being sent on another mission. I am not ready for that yet.'

Betty walked up to the reception desk.

"I am Betty Peterson."

The receptionist looked up with a sense of urgency in her face.

"Please go right in Miss Peterson, the chief is waiting for you."

Betty tapped on the door, and pushed it open to find the chief and Mr. Peterson in the room.

"Hello, chief, Mr. Peterson. I was told to report here on the double."

"Betty I have asked Mr. Peterson to join me. He had the tough assignment of getting you into the OSS, and it has not been fun and games for you, I know. But we may have some news for you that should make you happy for a long time. I will let Mr. Peterson explain."

Now Betty was even more puzzled as to the meaning of this meeting.

"Betty, we have hesitated to bring you up to date on this, but you have proven you can take disappoint-ments, so we are going to let you in on what we have."

"Yes, I think I can take the good with the bad."

"Betty about ten days ago we received a message from MI-6 in regard to Alamo. It is their opinion that maybe not all the members of this mission were killed. Some of the partisans seem to know for a fact that at least one of the team, and maybe two, escaped the hit. We did not put much credence in this, since we have not heard from any of them since that fatal day. We did learn from the FBI about a week ago that one of the team members was a German agent. There was an attempt through MI-6 to warn the team of the enemy agent being a member of their group. MI-6 did respond, however, it was learned later that this agent was a plant and probably assisted in the hit. It was not until this morning that we received what we believe to be a reliable confirmation that at least one of them has indeed survived. A British agent posing as an Italian officer in Naples had seen a young Italian working as a waiter in one of the restaurants in the Spacca-Napoli district. He felt that this man was on the run, and tried to reach him, but before he could make contact the young man had fled.

The agent in Naples was able to get some information from one of the waiters. He told our agent that this man had an uncle living in Andretta, a small village southeast of Naples. As soon as practical the agent in Naples had the partisans check out any newcomers to the little village. Many of the young men who are avoiding serving in the Italian army are hiding out in the rural areas. Because of this, any stranger asking questions is immediately avoided. A check into the newcomers around Andretta did reveal that a man who might fit the description of Tony had been there. A visit to the farm produced nothing. The owner refused to talk about this young man who was believed to be his nephew. The man who owns the farm is Papa De Angelo. Our contact made another visit to the farm, but he was also told that he had left the farm. (He never admitted that Tony was his nephew.) He was probably frightened by the sudden attention." Betty gasped, "Could it be that Tony was there?"

"Yes Betty, we believe that man to be Tony De Angelo. If this is the Tony we know, and he told his uncle that he had to go to America to save the life of a very important person, it would certainly indicate he planned to come home."

"We cannot understand what he meant by this statement. Could be that the uncle misunderstood what was said - but maybe he didn't!"

"Do you think Tony is coming back to the states?"

"Based on the information we have, and that information being reliable, it would seem that such is his mission. Tony is frightened and in this state he will trust no one. Of course the jack pot question is; how could he get back?"

"Betty we are going on the assumption that Tony is alive and is on the run. We will try in every way to find him and assist him in getting out of Italy. All we can do now is wait and see if our agents can make contact."

"You know I have never been told the purpose of Alamo. What were they suppose to do Mr. Peterson?"

"Betty this cannot go out of this room, it is top secret. Their mission was to take out the number one man in Italy."

"You have got to be kidding." She exclaimed.

"No, that was it!"

"Then how did a German agent come to the United States and become a mole in the OSS?"

"We are looking for the answers by the hour. Right now we are in the dark. Remember, not a word out of this room to anyone. From the time you came into the room until you leave, all that you have been told, including about Tony, must be kept secret. You see we don't know why the team was hit, or who Tony believes to be in danger here in the states. We don't know how deeply the OSS has been penetrated. If there are other foreign agents in the OSS, or the FBI, they will also be trying to locate Tony."

"I appreciate this information more than you will ever know. I want to believe that Tony is alive and will be back in the states very soon." Betty stated with genuine gratitude.

"Let's all hope and pray, Betty."

TWENTY - SIX

Tony was up at daylight observing the crowded roads. By all appearances the entire Italian and German armies were on the move. There just had to be an invasion to justify all this traffic. 'If it were really the Americans, not the British.' He thought wistfully.

As Tony got closer to the road, he could see that most of the trucks and drivers were from the Italian Army. He did not know at the time that Italy had surrendered to the Allies, but not all the Italian army did. Tony traveled off the road moving along in the same direction as the trucks. The trucks were headed somewhere and Tony would have to follow to satisfy his inquiring mind.

Late in the afternoon Tony arrived at the top of a hill where he could see the trucks pulling off the road into a wooded area. After some slipping and sliding he got close enough to see this was an assembly area. Gas cans were stacked by the hundreds - along with other equipment and supplies. The trucks he had followed brought in supplies, stayed just long enough to unload, then return. There were other trucks loading supplies, mostly "jerry cans", (five gallon gas cans) and heading toward the coast. These trucks were going in the direction of the gunfire, so he imagined that was where he could possibly make contact with the American Army.

Tony hastily devised a plan: unrealistic, impossible, reckless - yes! But, it was the only plan he could think of on the spur of the moment. If it didn't work, he could say he gave it his best shot - he tried.

He would have to become a driver of one of the trucks in a convoy. This would take him closer to the fighting and the Americans.

He decided to select the last truck in the convoy. It was getting dark - an ideal time to bush whack one of the drivers. He waited until the trucks started moving up front. The last few trucks were still idle, waiting for the trucks in front to move. He walked slowly to the rear of the last truck, bent down at the back wheel, and motioned for the driver to come and see. As the driver approached and bent over, Tony clobbered him over the head with a big rock. Tony quickly removed his clothes, pulling them over his own, then pulled the body into the cab of the truck just in time to move along with the convoy. He would get rid of the soldier somewhere along the road where he would not be found right away. He did not intend to kill the man, but there was no doubt now that he was already dead.

From talk he overheard from the drivers, this convoy was carrying gas to supply German tanks somewhere up ahead. The convoy, along with Tony's truck, moved along without a hitch. If no one asked him any questions then there would be no problems. Just as Tony was thinking positively about his masquerade, the convoy stopped. Maybe this would be a brief stop. Obviously it was a planned stop, since everyone was getting out of the trucks to stretch.

Tony could only think of one thing - get rid of the body. He pulled him into a ditch, covered him with brush, and quickly returned to the side of his truck just in time to hear someone up the road calling.
"Caffe? as he started walking toward Tony.
Tony's mind was racing with anxious thoughts: 'Where can I go? I've got to stall, but how?'
"Non capisco," pointing to the truck engine that was running, then to his ear.
"Caffe?"
"No! grazie." Tony started walking around his truck to the driver's side, hoping the man would take the hint. Was the man suspicious; he kept staring at him as though he was trying to place where he had seen him before. If he comes back here I'm a dead duck. As though an answer to prayer, the convoy started moving out again.

Some time later, after dark, the convoy pulled off the road again. He estimated there were at least one hundred German tanks and self-propelled guns in this one area. The tanks were being loaded with ammunition and gas. It was like a beehive, and Tony surely didn't want to be around his truck when it was unloaded, so he moved into the small trees on the edge of the holding area. Before he realized it, a

German officer had spotted him. He yelled at Tony;
"What are you doing out here, you are supposed to be
servicing tanks, not walking around!"

The German officer walked him over to one of the
maintenance sergeants, who was Italian, and ordered
him to put Tony to work. He was given a grease gun
and told to grease bogie wheels on the tanks. Tony
went about his duties with enthusiasm. As he worked
on the tank he could see another part of his plan taking shape.

From the conversations he overheard, he learned
of a large American attack from the beachhead during the day. They had taken some important posi-
tions from the Germans and the next morning the
Germans were going to take it back, then push the
Americans and British back into the sea.

On the morning of September 12th, which was
D+3, the German tanks rolled toward the beachhead.
Defending this sector were troops from the 141st
Infantry Regiment of the 36th Division. The Panzers
were overwhelming. They overran the American
forces, breaking through to reach within two miles of
the water. Many Americans were killed, wounded, or
captured. Having such success against the
Americans the German commanders decided to make
an all out effort the next day to eliminate the beachhead.

Another part of Tony's plan seemed to be materi-
alizing. If he could get into one of the German tanks,
it could take him close to the invading forces.

The German counterattacks started on September

13th. Some of the tanks came back for repairs late that afternoon. The Panzer IV was the most common tank being used by the German army. It carried a crew of five men: a tank commander, driver, gunner, machine gunner, and loader/radio operator. The tank weighed 20 tons and carried a 75mm main gun and two 7.92 machineguns. Tony had decided that the only position he might possibly fill would be the loader/radio operator, whose position was opposite the driver in the front of the tank. It would be a great risk, but what he was attempting to do consisted of multiple risks.

Tank motors had been running off and on during the night as the maintenance crews got them ready for the next day's attack. There were about thirty tanks ready to leave from the assembly area.

The morning of the 14th was rather cloudy, with a layer of fog shrouding the atmosphere, making visibility limited. Tony had selected one tank sitting along a small tree line. Tank crews were milling around their own vehicle, waiting for the drivers to test engines.

After careful observation he had determined which of the crew was the gunner. Tony walked into the small trees a few steps, then motioned for the German soldier to come to him. Asking him for a cigarette should keep him from becoming suspicious, since it was common dialogue in any army to ask for a cigarette. When the German reached into his pocket for the cigarettes, Tony hit him on the back of the head with a blow that would keep him out for quite awhile. Quickly dragging him further into the little trees, he ripped off his jacket, put on his cap, and stepped back into view by the tank. He had wanted his pants also, but too much time out of view might cause suspicion; besides in the tank no one would notice. He went to the tank, reached inside and picked up a helmet, earphones, and goggles. Putting them on might disguise him for a while anyway - just long enough for the tank to pull out. By sitting in the tank, he may not have to say or do anything.

Since he was now the radio operator, he would be expected to talk - which he could not afford to do. The radio was used mostly for receiving orders rather than transmitting. If he was put on the spot he could always claim radio failure. The tank engine was running noisily, so he felt his cover was adequate.

As he was breathing a sigh of relief, he felt a tap, tap on his helmet. He looked over at the driver who was pointing to his earphones. Tony knew that he wanted him to talk through the radio; he was sunk! Tony threw up both of his hands in a gesture of dismay. The tank engine idled down so the driver could be heard to say: "The radio." This time he was really was sunk! The only thing he could do now was run and just hope they missed him. Suddenly, as though a miracle, the tanks started moving out up ahead and rather than miss the battle his tank followed. Tony was able to breathe once more.

It did not take long for the German tanks to come under fire from American artillery. The tank fired the 75mm gun repeatedly. Each time the gun fired, Tony wondered if the tank had been hit. There were shells exploding in front of the tank, and on the side, in fact, it seemed the tank was in the middle of exploding shells. For the first time, Tony was scared. Maybe he had gone too far - he was not ready to die.

Abruptly the tank shook violently. Smoke began to pour out of the tank; Tony knew they had been hit. He pulled himself out of the tank. He could see the turret on the ground about ten feet away, with three crewmembers tangled in the twisted metal - all dead. The driver was still in his seat, appearing to be dead also. Maybe Tony was the only survivor. He crawled into a ditch to avoid falling shells. The German tanks had now moved out of the area; the shelling diminished. Three Panzers were knocked out in the same area. There was no sign of life from any of the tanks. He walked over to make sure the driver was dead, but discovered that he wasn't. He had a severe head wound and was semi-conscious. Tony pulled him out of the tank and propped him up against a small tree beside the tank's hull.

As Tony wandered aimlessly through the area he began to notice some men lying along the road with different uniforms than the Germans or Italians. These were American soldiers; he could not believe it. They had shoulder patches the shape of an arrowhead with a "T" in the middle. After a closer examination of the bodies it was obvious that they had been killed the day before. They were beginning to swell, and also smell.

It was time for Tony to take on a new identity. As

he looked at the bodies - selecting one about his size - he decided on a Sergeant, named Anderson. He gently removed the dog tags, putting them around his neck, then started removing his uniform. There was a letter from his girlfriend in Fort Worth, Texas. Sergeant Anderson had bled to death from a leg wound. It was difficult for Tony to remove all his clothing; he was leaving him an unknown soldier, naked and nameless.

So intent on what he was doing, he did not hear the German soldiers approaching. They were coming from the direction of the beach; probably deserters. They started searching the dead Americans for items that they could use, such as watches, etc. Tony was laying low in a nearby ditch hoping he would not be discovered. When the Germans came to the stripped body of Sergeant Anderson, they looked at each other, "the Italians have been here," and laughed.

It was getting dark when Tony heard tanks coming in his direction from the beach. He again hid in a ditch, and as the tanks got closer, he could see that they too were German. Were the Germans retreating, or had the Americans been pushed off the beach and the battle was over. If the Germans had won the battle, and the beach had been evacuated, then Tony's mission was over before it began. However if the Americans were forcing the Germans back, then he would lay low and wait. The area now was full of Germans. He had to remember he was wearing an American soldier's uniform.

All during the night the little road was full of

German vehicles moving away from the shore. Shortly after daylight, on September 15th, a definite change was noticeable. Shells began to fall all along the road around him, but the artillery was more concentrated around the assembly area a few miles to the rear. Tony had moved down the road where he could see for some distance, and to avoid the shelling.

It was midmorning when Tony saw a different type tank coming up the little road. It had a white star on the side with a few soldiers following along behind. They were dressed as the other American soldiers were, and they looked like him. They had to be Americans. The tank stopped and the soldiers fanned out along the road as though searching for something.

For the Americans to pick up Tony he would have to prove to them that he was Sergeant Anderson. This accomplishment would unite him with the Americans and a newfound safety, but would do nothing to get him back to Washington. There was only one way he could achieve this phenomenon; he had to be a badly wounded Sergeant Anderson. He raced up the road three hundred yards where the German tanks had been destroyed. Remembering that the driver was not dead, he could stage a convincing gunfight. The tank driver was alive, but barely. Tony fired a round into the driver, killing him; then fired a round from the dead German's pistol. He then redirected his pistol, aimed toward his lower leg and fired. The pain was so unbearable he passed out.

The infantrymen heard the shots and cautiously approached the area. "Here is a GI badly wounded," someone yelled, "Medic!"

The medic came to Tony and immediately tried to stop the bleeding. As Tony came to he was asked, "What happened?"

"I was coming down the road to meet you guys, when this German, that I thought was dead, fired at me, then I fired back. Don't know if I hit him or not."

"Oh you hit him alright; he's as dead as a mackerel."

Tony, felt faint and passed out again.

"This is a very bad wound, I'll give him some morphine; that will hold him until we can get him to the beach."

They loaded Tony onto a stretcher, put him on the rear of a jeep and started toward the beach. This waked Tony and in his confusion, tried to move off the stretcher.

"Just hold on Sergeant, you're going to be alright."

"What outfit are you with Sergeant?"

Tony tried to talk, but before he could get an answer out, one of the medics noted.

"He must have been with the 141st of the 36th."

"Yeah, the 2nd Battalion got hit hard."

Tony had to remember - the 141st, 36, 2nd Battalion.

The road was bumpy and difficult to navigate at times, but Tony could hardly feel the bumps. The morphine was kicking in. When they reached the beach he regained consciousness and asked one of the medics.

"Where am I going?"

"Sarg, your war is over. You are heading for a hospital in Sicily, then probably to North Africa, and on to the states."
Tony had made it! He was extremely grateful in spite of the pain.

TWENTY - SEVEN

Sergeant Anderson, as Tony was now known, received the second blood transfusion as the LCT(landing craft tank) carried him, and other wounded, to a transport ship waiting off shore. Stretcher cases were loaded aboard the transport with the efficiency expected of the U.S. Army Medical Corps.

A nurse and an aid were unwrapping the bandages from Tony's leg when he once more gained consciousness. Confused and groggy; he tried to sit up.

"Where am I? What's happening"?

"Sergeant Anderson!" a nurse said in a stern voice, "you must lay still."

Tony again muttered, "Where am I?"

"You are aboard an American ship. We are trying to treat your wound." She explained.

"Open your mouth! Do not bite the thermometer. Do you understand?"

Tony raised one arm with one finger pointing upward - indicating he did understand.

"It's 103 degrees," whispered the orderly.

"The doctor should be here shortly. I will be back as

soon as I can. Stay here with him until the doctor arrives."

It was some time later when the doctor and nurse arrived at Tony's bedside. The doctor reviewed his charts, and started asking questions at the same time.

"Sergeant Anderson; I am your doctor, Captain Wilson. How are you feeling?"

"My leg hurts," he answered in a weak voice.

"I know it does Sergeant. We are going to give you something to ease the pain in a few minutes." Patting Tony on the arm.

"Nurse, let's remove the bandages, and take a look at the wound." The doctor took a long look, stepped back away from Tony's bed and began writing on his chart.

"I want the sulfa increased, aspirin for his fever until it breaks, and he may have morphine every four hours if needed. His tibia has been completely severed and badly shattered. He will have to be watched very closely. There is a strong possibility that the leg will have to be amputated below the knee. Keep me informed of any change and I will check back in a couple of hours. Get him ready to go ashore to the hospital in Sicily. Sergeant Anderson I am going to give you a shot for pain, after you take these pills. The shot will allow you to rest. You are on your way to a hospital in Sicily."

For Tony days and nights were the same, but for the pain that awakened him, then a shot and back to dreamland. He stayed in the hospital in Sicily for twelve hours. It was decided that there was only a twenty percent chance that his leg could be saved. He should be sent directly to North Africa.

Tony waked up during the move.

"Where am I?" He asked weakly.

"You are on a ship heading for Oran, North Africa to the 7th Station Hospital."

The 7th Station Hospital was equipped with 500 patient beds. Severely wounded patients were transferred to this facility. Tony's condition definitely warranted special attention. There was a slim chance that his leg could be saved. The doctors in Sicily felt that the leg would have to be amputated below the knee when he reached Oran. However, the antibiotic had been doing its job, and the infection seemed to be reacting favorably.

In a review of Tony's case by several doctors it was concluded that Tony should be sent to the Walter Reed Hospital in Washington, DC. If his leg could be saved it would more than likely be accomplished in just such a state of the art medical facility. Without delay, Tony was moved to the outpatient ward and readied for a flight to Washington.

"Sergeant Anderson! This is your doctor, can you hear me?"

Tony nodded his head.

"We are sending you to the Walter Reed Army Hospital in Washington, DC. Your family will be notified, and will be able to visit with you on occasions. Won't that be good?"

For the first time since being wounded, Tony was

shocked into a conscious state. Family, he thought. I cannot permit this to happen, not a family reunion. My true identity cannot be known - and this would do it.

"I don't want them to know that I am in the hospital." Tony tried to sit up to emphasize his feelings. "I don't want them to see me in this condition - don't you understand?"

"We understand sergeant, but you will feel differently when you see your family."

Tony was so weak; he could offer no more resistance. Lapsing back into delirium, he kept mumbling to himself. "I cannot see Sergeant Anderson's family; Sergeant Anderson is dead. They will know I'm not their son. So cruel - can't find out this way. Got to get to Washington - - - November - - - assassination," he agonized over and over as he drifted in and out. His mind was so overpowered with the latest happenings; then, skipping over to his urgency to reach Washington and the assassination attempt, that his pain became inconsequential. His overall plan had worked to this point, but he must reach Washington, and the proper authorities.

Tony and several other patients were loaded aboard the hospital plane for the long trip to Washington. As the plane lifted off, Tony began to remember the many things that had happened to him since being attached to the OSS. He thought about Betty. Should he try and contact her when he got back? What about the Anderson family? How can I notify the right people about the assassination? Will they believe me? As the plane motors settled into an even roar, it was the last sound he heard until a nurse waked him for his medication.

"Are we there yet?" Tony asked groggily.

"No", replied the nurse, "we have several more hours to fly before we reach our destination." She could have added; you have several more pills to take before we land.

"Are you warm enough?"

"I could stand another blanket."

With another blanket and a warm bunk, Tony went back to sleep, still wondering what the future would bring.

TWENTY - EIGHT

It was the beginning of a beautiful October day when the big four engine plane sat down at the Washington DC airport. Most of the patients were awake and excited about arriving back in the good ole USA. With care and concern each patient was moved from the airport to Walter Reed Army Hospital. This was an immense hospital and for the first time in months, Tony had his own bed, enveloped in crisp white sheets with a fluffy pillow.

It was difficult to measure time, but to Tony it seemed he had been in this same ward for days. The nurses were very attentive and did everything they could to make him comfortable. There was nurse Martha Peters, a blonde from Des Moines, Iowa - who hovered over Tony with extra special attention when she was on duty. There was something about her that attracted him. Was it because she looked like Betty? Maybe it was her smile, or could it just be that Tony had not seen a good-looking girl for so long.

The doctors and nurses had attentively monitored Tony's vital signs daily, and making sure he was comfortable for several days. Next he was sent to

X-ray for the necessary pictures to prepare for surgery.

'Are they finally going to take my case seriously now and fix this leg?' Tony wondered. In the afternoon following the morning's x-rays, two doctors came to his bedside.

"Sergeant Anderson, we are going to try to fix you up. We are going to try a new procedure that we hope will give you some use of your leg - maybe even 90%."

"Do you think I will be able to walk after you get through with me?"

"Sergeant, we have every reason to believe we will have you walking again, with the addition of some metal in your leg."

"I sure hope you can," he said weakly.

"We are going to start you on a new miracle drug that will aid in healing. You will get the benefit of the greatest breakthrough in science in this century."

The doctors had only been gone a couple of minutes when a nurse appeared holding a syringe fronted by a long needle. She pulled back the sheet, went to the good leg and punched the needle into his hip muscle with gusto.

"Ouch," yelled Tony.

"You might as well get use to this Sergeant, you will get one every four hours until your operation, then the same routine afterward."

"What are you shooting into me?"

"It's called penicillin."

True to her word, Tony had a visit from a nurse every four hours night and day. The only time the needle didn't hurt was when Martha was on duty and gave him the shot. She would always give him a little love pat, or a little squeeze, when she removed the needle, making it a little more personal.

At long last Tony was scheduled for surgery on Wednesday at 9:30 a.m. He remembered little of the day's activities. He did remember getting back to this bed, but it wasn't until a couple of days later that he became aware of his surroundings. The pain was severe, and he had received so many shots he felt like a human pincushion. After a few days, time and places came back to him. Waking up one day he looked into the face of his favorite nurse.

"How are you feeling," a low, sweet voice asked?

"Fair," replied Tony.

"You are going to be alright now. It will just take time for you to heal."

All the effort Tony could muster in response, was a half smile. She wiped his forehead and pinched his cheek and smiled.

Tony wondered about Lt. Peters. Was she just being nice to him or was it more personal. One day while a patient was visiting with him the subject of Lt. Peters came up.

"Tony she's crazy about you. She is a kind and caring nurse alright, but you get most of the caring. She's got it bad for you."

"How in the world do you know that," asked Tony.

"You're the only one in the ward that doesn't know it."

Tony was flattered to know that such a good-looking nurse was smitten with him. As for his feelings, there was a good side and a bad side. The good side was, Tony was attracted to her. The bad side was, he still loved Betty. Tony was not really convinced that he was special, until one night after midnight, nurse Peters gave him a shot then kissed him briefly - "good night," she whispered. She would have gotten into big trouble, had she been seen. She was beyond caring about herself, for this man had captured her heart and she didn't care who knew it.

The long days and nights of convalescing proved to be a difficult time. Had it not been for Nurse Peters, it would have been intolerable. She made the difference. Tony could not wait until he was well enough to take her out. Of course officers were not permitted to fraternize with enlisted men, but that could be worked out.

"Sergeant Anderson, I have good news for you. Your mother and father will be here this weekend to see you; won't that be great?" exclaimed the head nurse.

Tony broke out in a cold sweat; he could only stare at the ceiling. What was he to do? When the Anderson's see me, the whole plot will blow. Tony worried and fretted about the coming visit of the Andersons. He finally came to a decision - he was not going to see them as Sergeant Anderson. He told the nurse that he was just not ready to meet his parents and that they would have to wait a couple more weeks.

"I am not going to see them and that's that!"

"We don't want you to get upset, and of course your parents don't want this either. We will contact them and ask them to put off their visit for a while. Will that make you happy?"

"Yes", replied Tony; "I am just not ready for that meeting yet."

Tony had to sweat out the weekend for fear the Andersons might come anyway. This was a terrible thing to bring on this family, but the stakes were much too high, and if necessary; the family would have to be hurt. The President of the United States was much more important than a few people.

Tony had not yet figured out how he was going to notify the authorities about the planned assassination. The time was running out and there was still no plan.

The ward was being decorated for Thanksgiving. November was at hand. What must he do. He could call the OSS and try to convince someone there about the coming crisis. If they sent an agent, how would he know but what this person was in on the assassination attempt? He had been caught in that trap before. He could tell one of the doctors; but would they believe him?

Nurse Peters was on duty the next day and stopped by Tony's bed to visit. She told him about an exciting event that was coming up at the hospital.

"The President's wife is going to visit the hospital before Thanksgiving and again before Christmas. She visits many of the bed patients and even talks to them."

"You mean she might come into our ward?"

"Sure, and if you think she should come into this

ward, I will try and get it arranged," she laughed.

After Martha left, Tony felt that this was a miracle, for what better way could he ever hope for than to inform the wife of the president of his impending danger first hand. If she would just come into his ward, he could do something to attract her attention - even if he had to fall out of bed.

Several days later the First Lady arrived at the hospital. The news of her presence traveled fast. The nurses toured the ward, making sure everything was shipshape, just in case she came into this ward.

Tony rehearsed in his mind what he would do, or say when the First Lady came by his bed. It was not clear how he would get his message to the proper people, or if they would even take him seriously.

Someone at the entrance to their ward yelled, "they're coming."

To the despair of all in the ward, the First Lady passed by Ward 8-A; Tony was stunned; he had not counted on this. Not only had his opportunity passed him by, but he recognized one of the secret service men who had previously served in the OSS when he was at the farm. Was he in on the plot to assassinate the President? Tony broke out in a cold sweat and began shaking as though having a chill. Barbara noticed. "What's the matter honey, are you sick?"

"I don't feel so good," he responded weakly.

"Let me get a cold pack, I will be right back."

Unknown to Tony, or anyone else in Ward 8-A, a miracle was in the making. The First Lady had planned to visit a family friend's nephew, thought to be in

Ward 7-A. When the mistake was realized the group headed for Tony's ward. Several Secret Service agents toured the ward before she was allowed to enter. Apparently everything was cleared, for presently she walked into the ward just ahead of the Secret Service group.

As they walked down the aisle between the two rows of beds, Tony tried to attract the attention of the President's Wife by waving his arms and calling her name. All he got in return was a smile and a wave as she kept walking toward the end of the ward. She stopped at one of the beds and spent a couple of minutes talking to a patient.

As they started to move toward the door, Tony's heart beat faster and faster as she slowly made her way up the aisle, then seeing that she was obviously going to pass him by he knew it was now or never. When she was directly adjacent to his bed, in one desperate effort, Tony lunged out of his bed onto the floor; crying in a loud voice, "They are going to kill the President!"

Everyone was in shock. What is wrong with this patient?

"There are German agents in the OSS that are going to kill the president!"

The Secret Service agents gathered around Tony as he lay on the floor, and at the same time trying to push The First Lady out of the ward. She refused to leave immediately. She stood looking down at Tony as though having pity on the poor soldier.

"You have got to believe me. I am an OSS agent and I

know that they plan to kill him this month; before Thanksgiving I am sure."

Several of the nurses and doctors had reached Tony, getting him back into his bed.

"Nurse, give him a shot to calm him down."

"I don't want a shot, I want you to believe me," shouted Tony, as he passed out.

In the meantime, the First Lady had been dutifully ushered out of the ward by her escort of Secret Service agents.

After the nurses had calmed Tony down he had a visit from one of the Secret Service agents.

"Sergeant Anderson, I would like to talk to you; do you feel like talking?"

"Yes I do! I want to talk to someone who will listen. I am not Sergeant Anderson; I am Tony De Angelo a member of the OSS. I have been in Italy on a mission and I know for a fact that there is a plot to assassinate the President. The operation is called ALAMO and it is to be carried out before Thanksgiving, of this I am positive."

"Well, we want you to know that we take very seriously your statement and believe me we will follow up on what you have told us when we . . ." Tony would not let him finish.

"You don't realize how many people might be involved in this plot, some are in the OSS and maybe in your organization also."

All those who heard Tony could have easily believed the poor man had lost his mind; just too much war.

"You get some rest and we will be out here in the

morning to take down your complete statement."
"I will be here," sighed a relieved Tony.

After the patients in Ward 8-A had settled down, and Tony was feeling the effect of his shot, Martha came by on the pretense of checking on him, however, the visit was really to ask him some very serious questions.

"Sergeant Anderson, who are you? You said your name was not Anderson, but Tony De Angelo, a member of the OSS. I don't understand what is going on. How could you be Tony De Angelo, a member of the OSS and Sergeant Anderson, a member of the US Army? How do you know someone is going to kill the president?"

As briefly as possible, Tony told the part of the story that might make sense to her.
"This is unbelievable, Tony."
"Don't you see Martha, they are going to try to get rid of me, and I am afraid."
"They can't touch you in here darling, I won't let them."
"You don't understand, one of the leaders of the plot is a German agent and some of his people will know about what I said today in this hospital. They will get rid of me, if I am not protected."
"You must get some rest. I will be on duty until midnight, then if you want me to I can stay all night."
"I wish you would. Don't let anyone give me a shot or any other kind of medication."
"I won't, you can depend on me, darling."
Finally, Tony went off to sleep and Martha returned to the ward office.

TWENTY-NINE

Nurse Peters made her final rounds and gave the nurse that came on duty the special orders. She filled her in on the shocking events of the day. It seemed harder for Martha to believe the double identity of Sergeant Anderson/ Tony De Angelo than any of the other shocking information.

"Do you believe him, Martha?"

"Yes, I do! He believes he is in grave danger, because of what he knows. He wanted me to stay on duty all night. He is afraid that someone might try to kill him before he could give the FBI the complete story."

"You don't have to stay here all night, I will look after him and you know no one will bother him while he is in this ward."

"Oh, alright, I'll go on home," sighed Martha, "if you promise to take good care of him."

"Don't worry."

At 0200 hours four men appeared at the nurses station. They claimed to have an order for the removal of Sergeant Anderson. They also claimed to be from the FBI.

"You can't come in here and take out one of our

patients without orders from the commanding officer of this hospital. This is highly irregular and I will have to call and get this approved."

"Look nurse, this is a priority case and it involves national security. We have authority over this hospital and everyone in it. We are working for the President."

"I don't care," exclaimed the nurse, "I have authority over who leaves this ward and who doesn't."

By now the entire ward was awake, listening to the disturbance, except Tony, who was still under the influence of the pain medication.

The four men rolled a stretcher down the aisle of the ward, stopping at Tony's bed. They lifted him off the bed, onto the stretcher, and started rolling him toward the entrance.

"You can't take this man out of this ward!" Yelled the nurse who was trying her best to stop the movement of the stretcher. By this time Tony was awake and trying to get off the stretcher. They put two straps around his body pulling him securely to the stretcher.

"Don't let them take me out of here; they are going to kill me, don't you see that! As Tony pleaded, one of the men put a wad of gauze in his mouth for a gag.

"I won't, I won't," exclaimed the nurse who had promised Martha that she would take care of Tony.

"I am going to call the police!" as she ran to her office. She was closely followed by one of the men who snatched the phone wires from the wall.

"Nurse you are making our job very difficult. We are

protecting this man and moving him to a place of safety. We don't want him harmed either. We are FBI agents and you had better not interfere with our job or you will be sorry."

'Are they telling the truth. Are these men really FBI agents trying to protect Tony? What can I do?' she panicked inwardly. By this time the stretcher, with Tony aboard, had rolled out of sight down the main corridor. She would always remember the look on Tony's face; it was that of stark terror.

Tony was loaded into a waiting ambulance. Not being familiar with the loading process, they had loaded Tony into the ambulance feet first with his head next to the double back doors. Two of the men got in the back with him closing the doors behind them. The ambulance roared from the receiving dock onto the city streets.

Tony knew that this was his last ride. These men were not FBI agents, they were probably from the OSS, sent by the Big Man. As Tony's mind went racing through the facts, he knew if these men did their job, he would never be seen again. There was one possibility that could change the outcome of this one-way trip. If he could get the back doors of the ambulance open he could push himself out onto the street. It might kill him, but at least someone would know of his death. There was a slim chance that he would survive the fall, and be rescued by someone sympathetic to his cause, but he had no other choice; he must get out of the ambulance.

Tony had no idea where he was; but the street

seemed to be a major thoroughfare. Without attracting the attention of his guards, he quietly eased the
latch on the back doors, then, waited for the vehicle
to stop at a red light; then as the vehicle lunged forward, he opened the doors and the stretcher shot out
of the rear end of the ambulance, hitting the street
with a heavy thud. Miraculously Tony remained conscious. Being strapped to the stretcher probably
saved him from instant death.

It was a dark night and the cars were traveling
fast up and down the street. Obviously no one would
expect a stretcher, with a man strapped to it, to be
standing in the middle of the street. When an oncoming car approached this scene, the driver didn't see
the object in the street until it was too late to swerve
around it, or stop. The brakes were applied, but in
vain. The stretcher was hit with a sickening thud.
The driver and his passenger jumped out and rushed
to the aid of Tony. The blow had been so intense they
thought him dead. One of the men in the ambulance
took one look at Tony and knew he was dead. The
ambulance pulled away as a police car pulled up to
the scene.

"What happened?" Asked one of policemen.

The driver and his passenger tried to explain the
freak accident, but they were unable to get control of
themselves, they were in shock. The other policeman
called an ambulance on his radio.

"Look! He is trying to raise his arm.

One of the policemen knelt down close to Tony and
said; "hang on, we have an ambulance on the way."

He saw that Tony was trying to talk; the policeman knelt down and put his ear close to Tony's mouth.

"Betty, Betty" he was whispering as though using his last breath.

"What did he say," asked the other officer.

"He just said, Betty, Betty; probably his wife or girl-friend, poor fellow. I don't believe he will make it - he is smashed up pretty bad."

The ambulance finally arrived. They loaded Tony up and asked the policemen. "Where should we take him?"

"The man that hit him said he fell out of an army ambulance"

"You mean they went off and left him in the street."

Everyone was puzzled about the whole weird affair.

"Well, I guess he is a soldier, so we should take him to Walter Reed; it's the closest military hospital."

The civilian ambulance pulled up to the gate. "Where is the emergency room?" The driver asked. When the ambulance arrived at the doors, a doctor and nurse snatched opened the doors of the ambulance, jumped inside and quickly administered aid with emergency equipment; but to no avail - Tony was dead.

The hospital declared Sergeant Anderson DOA. (dead on arrival) His body would be held in the morgue until his death could be investigated.

By early morning the events of the night had spread over the entire hospital. The Washington Post had gotten the news and had a reporter at the hospital wanting the straight story. One of the patients in Ward 8-A had called the paper giving them some of the details.

The OSS, FBI, and Secret Service, had been informed, but none had a complete story. The big question was; who was Sergeant Anderson, and/or Tony De Angelo. A check of fingerprints clearly revealed that the man listed in the hospital records as Sergeant Anderson of the 36th Infantry Division, is not this man.

The FBI was put in charge of this investigation. Since the OSS had been implicated in the charges, they would not be allowed to investigate themselves. The OSS was reluctant to jump in and identify this man as one of their agents until they could get more facts. The statement he had made in the hospital ward about being in Italy on some OSS mission was a clue for the FBI to start working on.

The FBI went to Mantis of the OSS, asking for help in his identification. Mantis tried to play this as some kind of a joke.

"This man has never been a member of the OSS," he said laughing.

Unknown to the FBI all records of Tony De Angelo's association with the OSS had been destroyed. The FBI could only assume that they were being told the truth.

The FBI then went to the hospital and talked with those in Ward 8-A. No new light was shed on the identity of Sergeant Anderson, or Tony De Angelo. As far as the patients knew, this man was Sergeant Anderson.

The FBI interviewed Nurse Martha Peters at

length. Her relationship with Tony had been more personal than anyone else in the ward.

"I never knew," she explained to the FBI, "that this man was none other than what his records indicated; Sergeant Anderson of the 36th Infantry Division. He came to us from Oran, North Africa. The last day he was here, he declared himself to be Tony De Angelo of the OSS. His activities of the last day in this ward were as great a shock to me as to everyone else. I talked to him late in the night after his attempt to warn the First Lady about the President's danger. He was afraid that he was going to be killed for speaking out about the assassination attempt. He did tell me that he was an OSS agent on assignment in Italy when he found out about the planned assassination of the President. He said that a German agent was in charge of the operation; a high-ranking officer in the OSS. He changed his identity so that he could get to the states. His wound was self-inflicted. It was his only method of return to the states. I believed him and I also believe he was murdered by those who were behind the assassination plot."

Two FBI agents were dispatched to the 7th Station Hospital in Oran, North Africa. From there they were to backtrack Sergeant Anderson's trail as far as possible; maybe to Sicily or even Italy.

A special request was made to the United States Attorney General for permission to wire tap the offices of the OSS. Highly irregular; but it was felt that such a drastic step was necessary. A charge had been made that the Washington office might have a mole working there, that in some way could be involved in the assassination attempt.

The Washington Post reporter went to the FBI; he would not give up on a possible hot story.

"There is no mystery here," explained an FBI spokesman. "The patient was being transferred to another hospital for psychiatric observation."

"In the middle of the night?" shot back the reporter.

"Middle of the night or day makes no difference. This is a twenty four hour hospital. Patients are moved whenever there is an ambulance to transport them."

"Doesn't seem reasonable," as the reporter walked toward the door.

"Sir! Don't make this story more than I have explained it to be. That is all we want printed - understand!"

The FBI was waiting for a report from their agents who had been sent to Africa, Sicily, and Italy. They were also waiting for a break from their wiretap. As of the moment the man called Tony De Angelo was a man without an identity. The OSS and the army disclaiming him would have been an acceptable solution to the case, except for one thing - a body.

THIRTY

It was a crisp beautiful November day in Washington, DC as Betty and Mr. Peterson went to lunch. Betty had hoped Mr. Peterson had some good news about Tony, and when he didn't, the obvious question - why the lunch?

"Yes, tell me why!"

"Don't you know that I am still trying to get you to marry me."

"If you buy my lunch every day, and it is as good as it is today, then I might reconsider your offer."

While they were enjoying lunch, a friend of Mr. Peterson, who was an FBI agent, came by their table and spoke.

"I was hoping to get invited to sit with you two nice people."

"I know what you want Mike," Mr. Peterson answered with a grin, " you really wanted to be invited by Betty."

"Well," spoke up Betty with her million dollar smile; "you are invited."

After ordering, Mike asked Mr. Peterson, "Have you heard about the strange case involving a supposed OSS agent masquerading as an army sergeant?"

They both looked puzzled.

"I am not supposed to discuss this with anyone in the OSS, but if I can't talk with someone who has been around as long as you have Mr. Peterson, then who can I have confidence in. However, I don't know about Miss Peterson."

"If I can be trusted, then so can Betty."

"Are you sure neither of you has heard about this case?"

"No, I haven't," replied Mr. Peterson.

Betty shook her head, "No, I am totally in the dark Mike."

"Well this fellow was in Walter Reed with a severe leg wound. The day the President's Wife visited the hospital ward, he jumped out of his bed, claiming the president was going to be assassinated by someone in the OSS. His name was Sergeant Anderson from the 36th Infantry Division, yet he claimed to be an agent from the OSS who had been serving in Italy. While he was in Italy he found out about the plot. He somehow got back to the states and revealed the plot, which according to him, was to be carried out in November, prior to Thanksgiving.

"What was the man's real name," asked Betty in a half gasping voice.

"I don't know; but if you are interested I will try to find out."

"Would you please Mike?"

Mike's partner came by and motioned for him to get moving in his direction. They had an urgent call.

"Do you suppose, could that be … ?" She dared not

mention his name.

"Now Betty, don't jump to conclusions. We have many agents in Italy as well as other places."

"I know, but I have this strange feeling."

The FBI agents previously sent to Africa, Sicily, and Italy returned with little to report. The hospital records showed that a Sergeant Anderson was wounded in Italy, was a member of the 36th Infantry Division while at Salerno, was evacuated to Sicily, then to North Africa, and on to the states.

After the briefing one of the agents probably expressed the frustration of the entire group. "If the OSS holds to their denial of this man as one of their agents, then we are back to square one. There must be a Sergeant Anderson, or this man Tony De Angelo was lying about his identity. Could it be that this soldier is AWOL?"

"That is what seems to be a good option. Yet we have no fingerprints on this Tony De Angelo. He was never in the army, navy or the marines."

"If he was never in the military how could he be AWOL," asked one of the agents.

The case of who was Sergeant Anderson had come to a virtual stand still. There were no leads, and really no real credibility to the whole idea of an attempted assassination.

It was 0300 hours when the wiretap paid off. Recorded, was this brief message.

Alamo will be postponed.

This came from the office of the Big Man, Mantis.

"This is no proof that Mantis is in on the plot."

"That's true, but it does give validity to the claim made by this "whoever", that such a plan was in existence and that Mantis knew about it."

It was decided to put a twenty-four hour tail on Mantis and wiretap his home phone.

"If we put enough heat on him maybe he will give himself away by trying to leave the country."

With a big puff on his cigar, the chief stood.

"It's time to bring in the OSS and see if we can work together and get this case solved."

As he walked toward one of the large windows, in apparent deep thought, he wheeled around taking the cigar out of his mouth.

"John! Get in touch with Mr. Peterson and bring him up to date. If this man Tony was ever a member of the OSS, I am sure Peterson will know."

At 0800 hours the following morning, two agents from the FBI walked into Mr. Peterson's office. After introductions were made the two agents got down to the business at hand.

"Mr. Peterson, we have been working on a very unusual case that involves the army and the OSS," while handing him a copy of the report.

"It's really hard to believe or verify, but we have one body with two identities. The reason we came to you is to determine the true identity of the deceased. We need to know if this man is Sergeant Anderson, or by his own admission, Tony De Angelo, OSS agent. We had the records checked and there is no record of such a man ever being a member of the OSS."

"I can tell you for a fact that such a man did work for

the OSS and he was sent to Italy on a top secret mission. We have not heard directly from him since he arrived in Italy. Is this man's body in a place where it can be seen?"

"Yes, we have the body at the morgue. He was badly bruised from the accident which caused his death, but if we can locate someone who knew him, his body is recognizable."

Mr. Peterson paused for a full minute.

"Gentlemen, I would like to invite someone else to go with us and I would appreciate it if you could allow me the time to contact this person to see if she is available."

"Sure, we can wait, or come back later if need be."

Mr. Peterson buzzed his secretary.

"Would you please get Miss Peterson on the phone for me?"

"Yes sir, I will."

A few moments passed.

"I have Miss Peterson on the line."

"Hello Betty, what are you doing that you can't hold until tomorrow?"

"Nothing, if you need me I can come right over."

"Would you gentlemen excuse me for a few minutes. I would like to talk to Miss Peterson alone. You see Miss Peterson was very close to this man; if indeed this is Tony De Angelo."

"Certainly, sir."

Mr. Peterson walked out to the receptionist in the lobby; "Will you have Miss Peterson come into room 205 when she arrives?"

"Yes, Mr. Peterson."

Mr. Peterson was still in shock, he had to get away from those agents and not show his emotion. Could this be Tony? If it was, what will happen to poor Betty? Facts cannot be withheld from her, she must know - if this is Tony. She is going to die. She has pined over this man for months, believing he would eventually come home to her. When she finds out he made it back to the states; only to die - without ever seeing her. It is just too cruel to think about.

There was a light knock on the door. Mr. Peterson walked slowly to the door and opened it.

"Hi Betty, come on in."

"What are we meeting in this room for, are you gong to propose to me again?" she said with a big smile.

"Betty, I wish it was that simple."

"What's the matter Mr. Peterson?"

"Betty, I don't know how to say this in a way that you won't be hurt. There are two men in my office from the FBI. They may have found Tony."

"You mean my Tony, where is he and when can I see him?" Mr. Peterson stood, looking Betty in the eyes, not moving a muscle. Betty could see the tension and stress on his face, which sent a cold chill immediately through her.

"What are you trying to tell me? Tony is alright isn't he?"

"Betty, there is a man in the morgue that might be Tony, however this is not a certainty. I have asked you to come to go with us to see if this man might be someone posing as Tony."

Betty had slumped down into a chair, chills ravaged
her body and her palms were suddenly clammy. She
didn't say anything for a long time; finally - "I am
ready to go."

Mr. Peterson took her by the arm and started walking
out of the room.

"Now Betty, let's don't jump to conclusions. This man
could be anyone. They didn't give me a description so
I have no idea if he even resembles Tony."

After a thirty minute drive, the limo pulled up to
the rear of the hospital. The FBI men told the receiving department whom they wished to see. Betty hung
to the rear of the group as they walked through the
door into the holding room.

"I want Miss Peterson to help make the ID. She
knows Tony De Angelo better than anyone."

Betty was still hanging back of the group as the
attendant pulled the drawer out revealing the body.
As the cover was pulled off the face of the corps, Mr.
Peterson gasped - he said; "It's Tony." He looked back
at Betty turning to walk out of the room.

"Is it Tony?" asked Betty shyly.

"Betty, don't look. You don't want to see him in this
condition."

"No, I must; I must see him and make sure."

Mr. Peterson took her arm as they slowly moved
toward the tray. Betty gasped. She went limp and
would have fallen if the FBI agents hadn't helped Mr.
Peterson hold her up. When she came to, she tried to
go and touch him, but they would not let her.

"Come on Betty, let's get out of here."

Betty started sobbing and shaking all over.

"I can't believe it! I won't believe it! He is not dead!"

Her words turned into uncontrollable, hysterical sobbing.

It was not until after Betty had been given a sedative, that she was able to walk. She never spoke a word as they drove back to the office.

Mr. Peterson had provided the identification the FBI needed. It was now up to the FBI to try and piece together what had happened to Tony and to fill in the many blank spaces of his mission.

Now that Tony had been identified as a member of the OSS, the investigation was now centered in Italy. Agents from the FBI and the OSS were at once dispatched to Italy in an effort to put the pieces together.

The next day, Betty came to see Mr. Peterson.

Mr. Peterson had never seen her the way she looked that morning. Her hair was neatly combed, but her face was drawn, no make up, and she spoke as though she was in a daze.

"I want to know what happened. Why was he killed and by whom? Was it because he knew too much? How could he have known about an assassination plot against the President?"

"Betty, there are a lot more questions out there than there are answers. I assure you that the OSS, and FBI, will continue to work on this case until we have all the answers. There is a team on the way to Italy to try and find some of the pieces to this puzzle as we speak.

"Will you let me know?"

Mr. Peterson took both of Betty's hands into his, and with all the compassion he could muster; "you know how much this has hurt me, and I will do everything in my power to make this as easy on you as I can."
With a cold and unemotional voice; "Thanks."

A few days had gone by before Betty accepted the reality of Tony's death. It had now become an obsession to find out the reason for his death. Was it neglect on the part of the OSS? Who was to blame?

She was now contacting Mr. Peterson every day, either by phone, or visiting his office, asking the same question,
"Have you heard anything from the agents who went to Italy?"
The answer was always the same.
"We have heard nothing. We have some of our best agents in Italy, and I am sure they will turn up something of importance soon."

A week later Mr. Peterson called Betty to his office.
"Have you any news, Mr. Peterson?"
"Yes, Betty I think we do. The agents are on their way back to the states and I am sure they would not be coming back unless they had the facts. They will arrive tomorrow night. We have set up a meeting for the next day. You are invited.

THIRTY-ONE

The room was filled with men and smoke when Betty, the only woman at the meeting, entered the room with Mr. Peterson.

"The meeting will be in order. We are here today to finalize the Anderson/De Angelo case. You are about to hear one of the most remarkable and unbelievable cases in the history of the FBI or the OSS. Let me first give you some background on the man who will address you in a few moments - Agent Greene, of the OSS. Agent Greene has been with the OSS since it's inception. He has already jumped into Italy and completed that mission, then on to Africa where he assisted in the takeover of the French Navy in Oran. He has worked very closely with the Italians who were opposed to Mussolini and wanted to overthrow his government. He is familiar with the operations in Italy, which made him the ideal agent to be sent there to find out the facts about ALAMO. We believe he has uncovered the previously hidden facts in this case, and he is now ready to share them with us.

"Agent Greene."

"Thank you sir. You are about to hear one of the most

remarkable, unbelievable, extraordinary, cases in the history of human dedication and commitment.

The mission ALAMO was set up for the purpose of assassinating Mussolini. It was thought that if this could be accomplished the war in Italy could be avoided because Italy would surrender if its leader was eliminated. However, this was designed as a distraction from a much more lethal operation, which was the assassination of our own president. It was set up by one of the high officials in the OSS, who we now know was a German agent, known as Mantis. For your information, this agent was found dead in his room this morning from a self-inflicted gunshot to the head.

The OSS sent three agents to Italy under the code name ALAMO. They were joined later by MI-6 and Italian partisans. They had established themselves in an area south of Rome and had made good progress as to how the operation would be carried out to a successful finish. Unfortunately one of the OSS agents was a German agent. This was discovered as the group moved to Miami for the trip to Africa, but one of the group, Colonel Mayhew, who discovered the German agent, was killed when his plane exploded off the coast of Florida.

Our agents had been in contact with us on a regular basis, then without warning, all communications with the group stopped suddenly. A follow up of MI-6 went into the area and confirmed that the group had been hit, and as far as they could determine were all dead. The OSS agent, Joseph Kite, who was the mole, tried to later join up with some of the partisans, but his identity was discovered and the partisans killed him. This was confirmed by one of their leaders.

Sometime later one of the MI-6 agents discovered an American working in a café in the Spacca-Napoli district of Naples. Before he could make contact the American had disappeared. It is now known that this man went to Andretta, the hometown of his uncle. When the uncle's home was visited some very interesting information was revealed. The uncle said that his nephew was Tony De Angelo, and that he had visited his farm for some time during the late summer of 1943; he gave some key information. "Tony is going to America to save the life of an important person" - is what he said.

From the uncle's farm, Tony went toward the coast where the invasion of Italy at Salerno had started. We could not verify what Tony did after that; he simply disappeared. What we now believe, although it borders on the impossible, he apparently got into the German army by some method, and made it to the coast. There he changed identity and became Sergeant Anderson; who had been killed. He then shot himself, or got someone else to do it, so that he could be picked up by the medics and shipped out eventually to the states. We tracked his movements from the hospital in Sicily, then to Oran, North Africa, and on to the states and Walter Reed Hospital. We feel certain that the man who left the shores of Italy under the name of Sergeant Anderson, was indeed, Tony De Angelo of the OSS. You might find this hard to believe, but it is true. This man accomplished the impossible, and is one of the great heroes of the war. Now I will turn the mike over to FBI agent, Wills."

"Thank you. I will be brief on the subject of Sergeant Anderson. He was a member of Company E, 141st Regiment, of the 36th Infantry Division. His outfit was in the invasion of Italy at Salerno. The regiment did have heavy casualties as they absorbed some of the heavy German counter attacks. Checking with grave registration they did have several bodies that could not be positively identified, most because of severe wounds. One sergeant we talked to did remember one strange case of a nude male body without dog tags. They did not think much about it since such violations had happened in Africa and they attributed it to the act of that type of civilian. We located the body, fingerprinted it, and had the prints sent to Washington for ID. These prints did match those on file under the name of Anderson. Tony simply took the uniform and dog tags of Sergeant Anderson of the 36th Infantry Division."

"Thank you gentlemen," said the OSS chief. "Are there any questions?" One man stood, introducing himself as a member of the President's Cabinet. "I have never in my life heard of such heroism and devotion to duty as I have witnessed today. This man is a national hero and must be recognized by his country. The President will be forever grateful and so will this country. I am going to recommend to the President that this man be given a full military funeral in Arlington Cemetery. That is the least we can do."

To that no one in the room disagreed. Betty was sobbing so hard she had to leave the room.

"Are we in touch with his family? We need to have them personally notified and invited to the ceremony."

The OSS chief acknowledged the request. "We will take care of that sir." He then leaned over to Mr. Peterson, and in a low voice,

"Pete can you take care of this?"

"Yes sir, I believe I can. It will take a couple of days at least."

"That's okay, just get it done."

Early the next morning Mr. Peterson put in a call for Betty.

"Betty can you come over to my office?"

"Yes sir."

"Miss Peterson to see you," came the voice over the intercom.

"Send her in."

"How are you feeling?"

"Oh, I feel alright, I guess; I am still in shock."

"After you left the meeting yesterday, it was decided that Tony will be buried in Arlington Cemetery. The President will of course have to approve it, but that's just a formality. He will be given a heroes burial."

"I just don't know if I can go through it," sighed Betty.

"We will have to locate Tony's family. Do you know where they might be?"

"His father worked in a dry cleaner's called the Sunshine Press somewhere in Chicago."

"That will give us something to go on. I'm sure the

Chicago police can run him down."

The next day the Chicago police called the OSS in Washington. Tony's daddy had died a few months back, and his mother was in the charity ward of City Hospital with a severe stroke. She was unable to talk nor remember at times who she was. She will never leave the hospital was her prognosis. The children were not in Chicago as far as the local police could determine.

Mr. Peterson again called for Betty.

"Betty, Tony has no family. I have suggested to the President's staff that you were the closest person to him and that you should be his immediate family."

This was just too much for Betty. Tears began to flow and her mouth quivered; "I can't do it."

"Betty, Tony would rather you be there to represent him than anyone. That man loved you and you know it!"

"Yes, he loved me and I loved him. What will I have to do?"

"Nothing but receive the flag as his next of kin."

"The ceremony will be day after tomorrow. It will be a dark day in November for this department. Mr. Peterson put his arms around Betty, trying to console her.

Mr. Peterson had notified the agents that had known Tony, and would like to pay their respects at the services. He knew they would want to be in attendance.

"Are you sure it will be alright for me to accept the flag? After all I am not a member of the family."

"Certainly it will be Betty. What person could better appreciate and honor this man than you."

There was a long pause as Betty dropped into deep thought.

"I cannot accept the flag. I just don't feel right about it. Such a valuable gift should go to his family. I will be at the graveside services; but only as one of the spectators."

"You are not bitter at the department, are you Betty?"

"No, not bitter, but maybe a bit put out, if you know what I mean. I just feel so cheated, short changed. What could have been will never be and I am deeply hurt. I don't blame the department, just this rotten war. Here was a wonderful man and now he is gone, and I doubt that his sacrifice will make a penny's worth of difference to the outcome of this weird war."

"Betty, you might justly say that about many who have died, and will die, in this rotten war, but Tony did a service that few would even attempt. Only one could have accomplished what he did."

"I know, and I am ashamed that I said what I did, for I know that everyone who dies in this war has made the ultimate sacrifice. There is nothing greater for one to do. But you don't understand - it hurts so much losing Tony," Betty sobbed.

ORDER FORM

Postal orders: Kay-Dot Publishing, LLC
714 Manor Dr., Oxford, MS 38655
Telephone: (662) 234-1970
E-mail: gowen2@dixie-net.com

Name: _____

Address: _____

City: _____ State: _____ ZIP: _____

Telephone: (_____) _____

Sales Tax:
Please add 7% for books shipped to a Mississippi
addresss.

(   ) copies of A Day in November